REVIEWS OF TH

By George Fillis

A HEART TO SURVIVE
first novel in the Collingwood Series

AN UNEXPECTED FATHER
second novel in the Collingwood Series

UNPUNISHED CRIMES
third novel in the Collingwood Series

BURDEN OF CONSCIENCE
fourth novel in the Collingwood Series

TO CATCH THE WIND
Texas Frontier Stories

Author's website:
GeorgeFillisNovels.com

Author's Note: the Collingwood Series should be read in chronological order and not as individual stand-alone titles because of the background of events, characters, and storylines.

George Fillis

BURDEN OF CONSCIENCE

fourth novel in the Collingwood Series

Burden of Conscience / George Fillis

ISBN: 978-1-7359372-6-7 (Print)
ISBN: 978-1-7359372-7-4 (eBook)

Printed in the United States of America
Publisher: Bluerock7, LLC.

Cover Design by Berge Design
Cover Photo: Photography by Travis Novitsky

To Karen, my beloved wife, best friend and editor. From our first kiss, every day has been a honeymoon.
And to Dr. Lew Spurlock, the brother I never had.

Contents

"Man plans, God laughs."
Yiddish saying

Conscience: the awareness that
one's actions are right or wrong.
Merriam-Webster

Prologue

The setting for the Collingwood Series finds 14-year-old Wen Shun in Hangzhou during Mao's regime takeover. When his father made public comments against Mao, his mother, Lil, a progressive schoolteacher, made arrangements through a feeder agent named Zhang to send Wen Shun and his sister, Lijuan, to Vancouver, British Columbia. Only Wen Shun is accepted and is "shipped" from China to Canada, along with other boys, to sponsoring Chinese families. But when they arrive, there are no families, only Dung and Tak, criminals operating a labor trafficking ring.

Wen Shun changes his name to Winson, hoping to assimilate. Conditions in the logging camp are terrible, and he and his friend, Kai, attempt an escape only to find the local police are taking bribes from Dung and returning escapees to the camp, where they're brutally punished. Finally, a black man named Jackson comes to work at the camp, and with his help, the three of them escape to Collingwood, Ontario.

They become good friends, find work at Collingwood's shipyard, and rent an attic room from Joseph Lawrence. Winson befriends a boarder named Catherine, a blind piano teacher who coaches him on life and helps him improve his English. She also introduces him to Virginia, a nurse working for Julian LeBlanc, a quadriplegic from an auto accident who owns Merchants Bank. Winson is hired as Julian's live-in caregiver. Unlike the shipyard conditions, LeBlanc treats him with respect, and they bond. Even his distrustful housekeeper, Rhoda, grows fond of Winson.

Winson meets Caitlin, one of Catherine's music students, and they fall in love. Her father, Kierian, is a shipyard supervisor who takes aggressive steps to discourage their relationship. Despite apprehensions about her father's acceptance, Caitlin marries Winson and is disowned by her father until he needs Winson's help to restore his reputation.

LeBlanc offers the newlyweds housing and continues to mentor Winson in banking. LeBlanc trusts him with his business interests and gives him more and more responsibilities. Taylor and Check, the CEO and Head Cashier, resent Winson because they view him as inferior and are jealous of his relationship with LeBlanc. When Winson discovers discrepancies in bank records, an audit is conducted, and Taylor and Check are charged with embezzlement and flee to the U.S. to avoid prosecution. LeBlanc sponsors Winson to become a Canadian citizen, later adopts him, and makes him President of the bank.

Winson and Caitlin's lives are devastated when Tak arrives in Collingwood, determined to settle old scores with Winson, and they question if they can ever get away from the traffickers. Winson is befriended by Ellen Jerome, a Parliament Member, who appoints him to an immigration committee to address illegal trafficking. Tak attempts to murder Winson but is killed by an Ontario Provincial Police officer.

With LeBlanc's assistance, Winson attempts to locate his family in China and discovers the cruelty of Mao's regime. LeBlanc passes away, and his attorney, Clive Owen, informs Winson that he has inherited LeBlanc's house and bank. With the ownership change, many depositors exhibited their prejudice, and there's a movement to withdraw funds from the bank. With the bank on the verge of collapse, Caitlin and her best friend, Kathleen, are kidnapped. It appears that Dung and

Tak are after Merchants Bank. The townspeople are divided; several try to help, while others, like Darvin Avant, owner of First Simco Bank, are against a Chinese man owning a bank in their town.

When Kathleen discovers her husband is behind the kidnapping to pay his gambling debts, she divorces him and moves in with Winson and Caitlin to help with their new baby, Catherine Aria.

Character List

- Winson (Tao Wen Shun) and Caitlin Mulroney LeBlanc: Catherine Aria, daughter
- Kai and Wei Lei: Collingwood friends
- Catherine DeVeaux: Blind Piano Teacher, Joseph Lawrence's house resident; married to Yves Marceau (Catherine's friend from European concert tours)
- Rhoda: LeBlanc's former housekeeper
- YeYe: Winson's Grandfather
- NaiNai: Winson's Grandmother
- Lil: Winson's mother
- Tai: Winson's father
- Lijuan: Winson's sister
- Kierian and Maureen Mulroney: Caitlin's parents
- Julian LeBlanc (Merchants Bank founder and Winson's adopted father)
- Clive Owen: LeBlanc's attorney; Bitsy Owen: Clive's wife and a psychologist
- Peggy Bailey: Merchants Bank's V.P.
- Oliver Taylor: former Merchants Bank President (wanted for embezzlement)
- Colin Cheek: former Merchants Bank Cashier (wanted for embezzlement)
- Ellen Jerome: Canadian Parliament Member
- Douglas Yonge: Canadian Parliament Member; Immigration attorney
- Chief Kirkpatrick: Collingwood Chief of Police, Ontario Provincial Police

- Darvin Avant: First Simco Bank and Trust CEO
- Lysa Wu: Chinese girl who Dung trafficked into prostitution
- Dung: trafficking ring boss
- Chukee: Dung's mentally challenged brother
- Tak: Dung's deceased partner
- Eng: Dung's right hand man after Tak's death
- Zhang: trafficking ring's Hangzhou feeder agent

Chapter One

Collingwood, Ontario | January 1967

I was in a cold sweat during the fourth watch of the night and looked up at a long stone wall, at least twenty feet in height, with thorny shrubs along the base. I walked until I came to a pair of tall wooden doors shaped like praying hands. My head was spinning as I stumbled toward the doors and, with blood-stained hands, grasped the cold steel handles and pushed. The door groaned but didn't move until I braced myself, leaned forward, and pushed with all my strength.

The wind howled past me through the open door, and before me was a long narrow ascending road outlined by tall cypress trees. Stars were visible in the sky above, and at the road's end was a house that resembled my Hangzhou home. As I approached the house, the trees swayed, and shadows fell across my path. Then, when the wind stilled, I heard familiar voices repeating, "Help! Oh, who will help?"

I searched in the direction of the voices and saw two figures emerge from the crest of the road running in my direction. I bit my lip as I recognized my mother and sister flailing their arms and yelling for help.

Then I heard another voice from farther away. At first, it was faint and unintelligible, then louder and closer, and progressively the words became clear.

"Winson, wake up! Are you okay? Winson, you're dreaming."

I bolted upright, my body trembled, and my vision blurred, so I rubbed my eyes, slowly opened them, and looked around. Caitlin had her arms around me, whispering my name. The dream was so real I expected to see my mother and sister, but the two figures and my home in Hangzhou were gone.

"You're shaking, and your clothes are soaking wet. Let's get you in a hot shower and into dry pajamas. You've had another nightmare."

"I keep having haunting dreams about my family in China. I was in Hangzhou this time, saw my mother and sister, and even heard their voices."

"What did they say?"

"Will you help us?"

"You're at home with me and Aria. We're here for you. Take a few deep breaths and try to relax."

Caitlin was my guardian angel, always watching over me. Her touch was warm and comforting as she lifted my shirt.

When I showered and returned to bed, I tossed and turned until Caitlin said, "You obviously can't sleep and neither can I. Do you want to tell me more about your dream."

I closed my eyes, centered myself, and told her what I saw, but the most frightening part was when my mother and sister yelled for help and I had no voice to answer. I tried but nothing came out, and then Caitlin was next to me, waking me up.

As Caitlin held me in her arms, I asked, "What does it mean?"

"Dreams come from your sub conscience and don't necessarily have meaning."

"I've tried to find my family. What more can I do?"

Caitlin put a hand on each side of my face and said, "Love, be calm. You've done everything you can. You know how things have changed in China."

I held her in my arms and let the air out of my lungs with a groan.

She gently stroked my body, kissed my neck, and whispered in my ear, "Since you're back among the living, how about a little morning delight to take your mind off those monstrous nightmares?"

She completed my world, and I lived for her and our beautiful daughter, Catherine Aria.

∽

While Caitlin and Kathleen cleaned the kitchen after our Saturday evening meal, I read to Aria in my easy chair before a warm fire. She smelled of baby powder, and her skin was as soft as a day-old chick as she snuggled in my arms. Despite my animated voice, she was fixated on the flames and glowing embers as they broke loose from the burning logs and rose like fireflies in flight. Watching her little eyes glow with fascination, I was filled with joy. She was a gift, a treasure to behold.

From her birth, I watched the way Caitlin held Aria and cradled her in her arms. So tender and loving was the bond of trust between them, it gave me a new perspective of how my mother and father raised me. Mother would enjoy knowing she had a granddaughter and revel in nurturing Aria, like she and YeYe nurtured me and Lijuan.

Aria was mesmerized and playing with YeYe's Ivory medallion hanging around my neck when the doorbell rang.

"I'll get it," Caitlin said.

Our front doorbell was Westminster chimes and Aria loved the sound. She was babbling when Caitlin came into the parlor.

With a tremble in her voice, she said, "There's a huge Chinese man, speaking Mandarin on the porch. He raised his arms and said your Chinese name, Tao Wen Shun, several times. I know it's freezing cold, but I didn't want him in our house, so I motioned for him to wait on the porch."

From the look on Caitlin's face, the memories of Tak attacking us in the Ottawa train station and his attempt to kill me in Collingwood had to have been on her mind. "Take Aria, and I'll see what he wants.

Aria leaned away from Caitlin as she gripped my medallion. Gently removing her fingers, I handed her to Caitlin's waiting arms.

"Do you want me to call the..."

"No, no. If he meant to harm us, he would have pushed you aside and forced his way in. Maybe he's one of Kai or Wei Lei's friends from Timmins. Let me see what he wants."

She took hold of my arm to stop me, bit her lower lip, and swallowed hard.

"I'll be careful."

I kissed her and Aria on their foreheads.

Caitlin had switched on the porch lights, and a frigid wind swept in as I opened the front door. The man standing on the porch filled the doorway and had his back to me. When he turned around, I recognized Eng immediately. The last time I saw him was at my bank with Dung, and he carried a suitcase filled with $100,000 cash. He had gained a few pounds, and his course black hair was greased back and tied in a ponytail. He was an intimidating figure in a fur-lined parka and leather boots, and I had been subjected to his abuse many times in the logging camp. From his dress, his position had significantly changed for the better.

Chills crept up my spine, and not from the bitter cold, as I grabbed my coat from the hook and closed the door behind me. I didn't want him to see Aria, and feared he might have others with him.

I tried to keep an eye on the man in front of me as I carefully looked around to see who else might be lurking.

Eng said in Mandarin, "I am alone and here to deliver a letter to you. Can we go inside?" He looked at the front door, but I motioned for him to sit in a chair on the porch. When he walked, he thrust out his chest like a soldier on parade, and the chair compressed when he sat. He pulled an envelope from his inner coat pocket and handed it to me.

The letter was written in Mandarin, and I looked at the last page to see who had signed it. And when I read *Dung*, I looked at Eng as he shifted in his chair.

Not knowing what to expect, I sat and read:

> *My little shoemaker,*
>
> *Thanks to you, I am living in isolation outside of Canada. I am in my last days, and my body is wearing out. What I am experiencing is not something I would wish on my enemies. Death is pursuing me, and I will not be able to elude it.*
>
> *Under desperate circumstances, I have been forced to carry out many evil acts in this world, and the gods are now evening the scales. In my youth, my family and I were tortured and brutalized at the hands of the Japanese. There were many situations that I should never have survived. But I have a strong will to live.*

I hope my father would be proud of how I cared for my family and kept them alive under dire circumstances.

I sense a strong spirit in you. There were many opportunities to have taken you out, but I'm the one who stayed Tak's hand, and when he went against my orders, he paid the consequences and got himself killed.

You and I could have been great partners. Instead, you blamed me for your wife's kidnapping even though I brought you the ransom money you desperately needed to keep her alive, and all I asked was a stock interest in your bank. I was innocent, my hands were clean, and I gave you $100,000 in cash, but you did not return my money.

You still owe me! But I have a proposition for you.

My brother, Chukee, cannot take care of himself. He is terribly ill and entirely dependent on me. He will not live long past my time. You know his condition, and because you, above all others, took an interest and showed him kindness, he favors you.

When I asked him where he would like to go when I leave this world, he says "Instrument." I know that was his name for you, and that you could take care of him for the remainder of his short life like you did the banker. None of my men could care for him.

I'm not expecting you to do this without compensation. I will provide several things. First, $50,000 for you to use to provide for his medicine and personal care. Any cash remaining after his passing belongs to you. Second, the $100,000 ransom cash I provided you with is now yours with no strings attached. Third, I have connections to find and return people close to your heart.

I held the letter and paused, thinking about who he could be referring to. The only people I wanted to see alive, besides my family in China, were the couple who assisted my escape from the camp.

"Are Suk and Biyu alive?" I asked.

His face saddened as he said, "Suk was a good man, but Tak cursed him."

"Are they still alive?"

He wouldn't look at me, but when we made eye contact, he shook his head.

"They risked their lives to save mine." I said with a heavy sigh. "I would have offered my life to save them."

"Suk and Biyu were dead as soon as they helped you. Dung and Suk were friends and came from China together as equals. Tak had no problem with blood on his hands and looked for an excuse to kill Suk."

Eng confirmed my fears, and I closed my eyes and looked away. When Eng cleared his throat, I refocused, lifted the letter, and continued reading.

> *It is nearly impossible to find and extract family members who are still in China, and the only tactic that goes undetected by Mao, and has worked in every society since time began, is bribery.*
>
> *I have gold in China to pay officials who are reasonable, and a network of contacts who can traffic people out of China, like those who helped your family, and brought you safely to Canada.*

I detested his reasoning and how he manipulated events, but I also knew from Howard Wong's reports that his comments about China were correct.

> *I hope to locate your mother and sister and bring*
> *them to Canada so that they can live out their lives with*
> *you in Collingwood. Unfortunately, your father is a*
> *political prisoner, and I am unable to get him released.*
>
> *I sent Eng to present this proposal and to receive*
> *your reply. Shoemaker, I cannot wait long for your*
> *answer, and you will never see me again. This is your*
> *only opportunity to save your family.*

> *Dung*

I dropped the letter on my lap and stared into space. A glimmer of hope resurrected, but at the same time, doubt over whether Dung's proposal was even feasible, and if he could carry out such a plan? The situation in China worsened every month due to Mao's oppressive policies, but if Dung could find Mother and Lijuan and bring them to Canada, it was certainly worthwhile because they had no connections or resources on their own. Dung was laying that possibility before me.

Eng lit a cigarette, and when the odor filled my nostrils, I was nauseous, as the smell reminded me of the overwhelming dread that consumed me when I was in Dung and Tak's presence. With Tak's death, Eng must be Dung's new right-hand man. I knew him as a brutal guard who hung me on a pole like an animal carcass. When he suffered a spider bite, he begged me to treat him, and I doctored his wound. He didn't say a word of thanks or change how he treated me, except when he saw Kai and me attempt to escape, he rubbed his arm and turned away instead of turning us in.

"Where is Dung?"

"He is dying. You saw how he coughed up blood during his visit to your bank. His condition worsened, and he saw many doctors, who all said he had lung cancer and there was nothing they could do but give him drugs for the pain. He has no appetite, his clothes hang on him, he even quit smoking. Look at this."

He'd been fiddling with a cigarette case and handed it to me. It was Dung's gold case with his initials engraved on the top. He took a long drag on his cigarette, flicked the ashes on the porch, took another drag, tossed the butt in the yard, and said, "If Dung were an animal, we would put him down." He coughed several times. "He saved my life when he brought me with him to Canada, so I owe him." He used his thumb and forefinger to pull the loose tobacco from his tongue and lit another cigarette.. "Are you going to take care of Chukee?"

I looked off into space for a few minutes, then said, "Come back tomorrow morning, and I'll give you my answer."

"I respect you for standing up to Dung and Tak and I am surprised you survived." His voice softened as he said, "I could not thank you for healing me because of Tak. The best I could do was look away when I saw you and your friend heading to the fence to escape. At the time I wished it was me. Even though it is long overdue, I want to thank you now."

"It's never too late, and I appreciate what you did for Kai and me."

"Dung is the only one who can rescue your family from Mao, but you must decide before he dies. Trust me, after he is gone, things will change under the new boss."

"I'll talk to my wife first and see you tomorrow morning."

He stared at me, then put the gold cigarette case in his pocket. The chair groaned under his weight as he stood, and I watched as he lumbered along the walk.

Aria was asleep in Caitlin's arms when I returned to the parlor.

"You were out on the porch a long time and look as though you've seen a ghost," she said.

"Put Aria to bed and I'll tell you what happened."

When we were alone in our bedroom, I told her about my conversation with Eng and read Dung's letter to her.

She was deep in thought for a few moments, her fingers rubbing her face in a worried fashion. "What are you going to do?"

"Not me, we. This is a decision we need to make together."

"We need to include God in this decision. Can we pray together?"

"Certainly. There are many known and unknown consequences in what we decide."

She prayed for wisdom and a sense of peace about whatever decision we made. I thanked God for blessing me with the best wife a man could ever ask for and also asked for me to be able to hear Caitlin's heart. I laid next to her as she fell into a quiet sleep, but I tossed and turned until I could no longer remain in bed. YeYe taught me that if you're stuck, you should pause and wait for an answer. I arose and went into my office to wait.

I opened the file with Wong's last letter and reread about deteriorating conditions in China and his telling me that he couldn't continue searching for my family. I thought I had accepted the fact I would never see my family in China again, but Dung's letter rekindled a longing. Could my heart withstand another disappointment if the rescue failed, or worse, if they were tortured and killed during Dung's attempt to get them out of China?

What if this was an evil tactic? In Dung's world an eye for an eye was one of his for two of yours. He never bargained for an even exchange. And his reference to not receiving stock in the bank could be an indication of his intention.

My thoughts turned to Caitlin and what it would mean for her to have Chukee, and maybe Mother and Lijuan, living with us. Caitlin had been so happy since Aria's birth, and we had talked about trying to have another child once Aria turned one, but how could I turn my back on my mother and sister? I kept cycling back to it being a joint decision, and not mine alone.

∽

It was early morning when Caitlin came into the study with a cup of hot tea. She put her hand on my shoulder and kissed my cheek. Her touch was soft and her smile warm. "What time did you get up."

"I couldn't sleep. I'm worried about the impact this could have on you, our family, and our marriage."

"Love, our marriage is strong. We talk to each other and confide in one another. This is your mother and sister. You have to try and get them out of China. Sure, things will be difficult, but as long as we keep talking and sharing our feelings, we'll get through this."

"What about Chukee? We'd be committed to taking care of him for who knows how long."

"Dung's giving you enough money to hire help and fortunately this is a big house. I won't be able to take care of him and Aria too. And you still have the bank to run."

"I've been trying to compose a letter to Dung, but I won't send it without your approval."

"Tell me what the letter says. I'm sure you wrote it in Mandarin."

"I told him I appreciated his efforts to save my family and would take care of Chukee, even if he hadn't offered to deliver my sister or mother in exchange."

"I would've been surprised if you had answered any other way."

"It's who I am. Dung could have killed me several times, but he didn't. He understands how much I want to get my family out of China because like me, he survived against all odds fighting to save his family. Writing this letter, I feel like I'm trying to catch the wind. Is all this an illusion?"

"I don't think so. Eng was on our front porch last night, and Dung's letter is real. What else did you write?"

"I thanked him for safeguarding my life and said I would pray for his soul."

She swallowed hard, and her eyes widened. "So, what are you going to do?"

"My life has been full of the unexpected. But there has always been a north star to guide my way. I received kindness from the most unexpected sources, like when Eng allowed us to escape. I hope by his hand, once again, there'll be another escape to freedom for Mother and Lijuan."

I covered my mouth with my hand and felt my heart in my throat. "I trust that the holy man in Hangzhou, in honor of YeYe, is moving Dung to help YeYe's daughter and granddaughter. As Dung fears the end of his life perhaps he's feeling his conscience. With your approval, I'll accept Dung's proposal."

She took me in her arms and whispered in my ear. "How you responded to all that has happened to you is because of how you were raised. You have noble character. I love your heart and support this decision one hundred percent."

Chapter Two

Eng didn't show up the next day. I told Caitlin there must have been a change in Dung's condition, or Eng would have been here. I tried to put the conversation with Eng and Dung's letter out of my mind because I didn't want to go through a repeated cycle of hope and despair.

A few weeks later on a Sunday morning, light snow had fallen during the night, and there was a chill in the air. Caitlin, Kathleen, and Rhoda had gone to church, and I stayed home with Aria. She was bundled in a warm jacket, and I held her in my lap on the porch swing, rocking and singing. When the wind kicked up, I looked around and saw empty streets and snow piled along the sidewalks. When the birds chirped, Aria cooed, so I started singing and rocking again. It was a moment of pure pleasure until a black Cadillac pulled up along the front curb and stopped.

The driver's door opened, and Eng appeared wearing the same parka over dark shark-skin slacks. He sported a fur-trapper hat with fox trim as he opened the trunk, pulled out a black leather briefcase, and came up the stairs.

I motioned for Eng to wait while I carried Aria inside. She cried and raised her arms toward me when I put her in her playpen, so I handed her a couple of toys that captured her attention and turned on her mobile. I wanted her inside while I met with Eng on the porch.

Eng had taken a seat, and after I sat, he said, "Shortly after I was here a few weeks ago, I received a call to return to Dung's bedside as soon as possible. He died two days ago."

The force of Dung's influence was over, and I hoped his death would put an end to human trafficking, sex slaves, and drug mules, but Eng had already said there would be a new boss, and the trafficking ring was larger than Dung and Tak. I was surprised at how my feelings wavered and took a moment before speaking. "I knew there must have been a change in his condition."

Eng looked away as he said, "It was gruesome. His lips, skin, and fingernails were blue. He had difficulty breathing and eventually lost consciousness. Of course, we gave him opium, but no one deserved such a death. I was the only one with him at the time of his passing."

Eng pointed at the briefcase and said, "Dung's last request was for me to deliver this to you." He laid the briefcase on the table and opened it. It was full of bundles of banded money.

"Why bring the money when I haven't answered you?"

"It is too late for that. Chukee is in the car and was told you would take care of him."

I pushed back in my chair and stiffened.

"This cold is not good for him. If you do not take him in, he will die."

It was like Dung to exert his will, force uncomfortable choices and circumstances, and have the last word. "Bring him in the house."

I closed the briefcase, set it inside the door, and returned to help Eng. He had removed a wheelchair from the trunk, opened the rear door, and lifted Chukee's limp body, which he gently placed in the wheelchair, then rolled him to the bottom step. Chukee smiled when he saw me and reached out his withered hand. I took hold of it and faintly heard him speak in Mandarin, "Yiqi" *(Instrument)*. His dark eyes were filled with pain, his face was flushed, and his head tilted to the right. His condition was worse than I expected. It took effort for Eng and me to lift the wheelchair up the five stairs to the porch, and I realized handling Chukee would be more difficult than I envisioned. I held the front door open as Eng pushed him into the house.

"Chukee, welcome to your new home. We're happy to have you here."

Chukee watched Eng go outside, then looked about his new surroundings and pointed toward Aria in her playpen. She stopped playing and looked curiously at him, so I pushed him closer to her.

"Let me introduce you to Aria, my daughter." She was looking at the two of us with big round eyes.

"Arrria," he said as he smiled at her. Chukee said a few words in Mandarin, and Aria smiled and was inquisitive at the sound of his garbled voice.

When Eng returned with two suitcases, he said, "One case has his clothes and the other his medicines and instructions for his care." He handed me a folded sheet of yellowed paper.

The hand that wrote the note must have been shaky because the Chinese characters were difficult to read.

> *My account with you is even. Thanks for looking after my brother.*
>
> *Dung*

"Your mother is being transported to Hong Kong to board a ship to Vancouver. I will contact you when she arrives," Eng said.

"What?"

"Your mother is on her way here."

The atmosphere was surreal. Even with the correspondence from Dung, his words caught me by surprise. It was as if Mother had risen from the dead. I was astonished Dung had actually found her through his contacts, and somehow got her out of China. In my mind, Dung had been a monster, and now perhaps, he was the savior of my family.

"Wow! Dung arranged this even without my answer?"

"He knew you would say yes. All his efforts in the last few months, besides spending time with Chukee, have been to locate and transport your family."

"What about my sister?"

"She is the favorite concubine of General Lin Biao and our contact is having difficulty."

"But Dung said..."

"I do not care what Dung said. If we cannot get her out soon, it may not happen."

"Okay. Will you bring my mother here?"

"No. We will first need to process her paperwork."

"Then she'll be arriving legally?"

"Best not to ask such questions. I will let you know when she arrives and you can come to Vancouver."

"Where will I pick her up?"

"Maybe from an island off the coast. I will let you know. We moved our operations offshore because we are getting too much heat from the RCMP."

"Why not bring her to Collingwood? I'll pay you."

He shifted in the chair, rubbed his face as he looked around, and said, "I have other responsibilities now and will not be returning to Collingwood. It is not my decision. Now that Dung is dead, another boss tells me what to do. I am responsible for the southern region, but he controls the province, and I must follow his orders. Dung did as much as he could before he died."

"Will the new leader stop you from bringing my mother and sister?"

"Maybe. Your mother is en route so chances are good she will arrive in Vancouver. Dung told the new boss his wishes, but the boss can always change his mind."

"Is the new boss in Dawson Creek?"

"If I tell you, I am dead and you will never see your mother or sister."

I was stunned by these circumstances and didn't trust the syndicate. My mind returned to the day the Dawson Creek men arrived in the logging camp. They dressed professionally in pin-striped suits and fedora hats, which didn't fit the surroundings, inspected each of us as if we were livestock, selected all the Korean boys, and loaded them in a cargo truck while the bosses rode in black limousines. I understood Eng was under orders, and I wanted to get Mother and Lijuan away from the syndicate as soon as possible but didn't want to go offshore for her because too much could happen, and I wouldn't have protection.

"With Dung and Tak dead, why don't you leave the syndicate and start over?"

"You saw how it was at the camp. Once you are in, you cannot leave. When you accept favors from men like Dung and Tak, you close a door to the life you had. Dung was good to me and I owe him my life, but when you lie with a dog, you get fleas." There was sorrow in his eyes.

"But now you have a chance to leave the syndicate. There's good in you."

"What good?"

"You let me go, and you saw the goodness in Suk."

His chair wobbled as he moved around, and he rubbed his thigh but didn't respond.

"Listen to the voice in your head."

"What voice?"

"Your conscience. It starts as a whisper, and if you listen, it shouts. It emanates from your heart which wants you to be free."

"It is too late for me. Besides, if I switch..." he moved his hand across his throat in a slicing motion.

"It's never too late."

"You have no idea what they do to control us. Know this, with my new boss, I will not be able to look the other way again for you."

"Your boss uses manipulation to control you. We all make decisions we regret, but you need to be able to live with yourself."

Eng's face turned red as he pulled his shoulders back and puffed out his chest. "If I left the syndicate, they would find me and make me dig my own grave. Tak suspected that I let you escape. He said I pushed boundaries, cost him, and had to pay." There was anger in his voice as he held up his left hand. The tips of his two middle fingers were missing. "I don't owe you anymore."

"Tak cut off the end of your fingers?"

"He tied an old cloth around my fingers, then made me do it. Everyone pays for their mistakes. I warn you now, Tak was a lamb compared to this new boss." He put up his hand in a stop motion. "Dung made the arrangements for your mother to leave China before he died and made me promise, if you took care of Chukee, I would get her to you. If we get your sister out, I will fulfill my obligation to Dung."

"Thank you for upholding your promise, and for bringing my family to Canada. You're an honorable man, and I'm the beneficiary. I hope you consider leaving the syndicate if you ever have the chance."

"I will be in touch."

"How do I communicate with you?"

"You do not."

"What if I need to call you?"

"For what?" He slapped his hands together and obviously didn't want me to know how to contact him.

"More medicine."

"There is enough medicine for months in the suitcase, but he will die before you use all the drugs."

"I don't even know Chukee's real name, can you leave me any identification papers for him?"

"Chukee doesn't have papers."

"So that's it! You just drive away until I hear from you again?"

"Yes."

He put his beefy hand on Chukee's head. "You take care little man. You are in good hands." He turned and walked out the door.

Chukee watched him and gave me a long, doleful look.

"Aria likes singing. Do you know any songs?" I asked in Mandarin.

He was singing a tune when I heard Caitlin, Kathleen, and Rhoda come in the back door.

Aria was jabbering when Caitlin walked in saying, "You're singing to her in Chinese! She likes…oh my!" She looked stunned as she uttered, "You must be Chukee."

Chukee looked at her but said nothing.

"Caitlin, this is Chukee. He only speaks Mandarin so I'll translate."

As I spoke in Chinese, he nodded, smiled at Caitlin, and said in Mandarin, "Laopo Yiqi."

"Laopo means wife, and Yiqi is what he calls me. It means instrument."

"Why does he call you Instrument?"

"Because of my xiao, and I told him I made musical instruments with my grandfather."

"We're glad to have you here, Chukee. This is your home now." After Caitlin spoke, I translated for Chukee.

We didn't know Chukee would be in a wheelchair. I'd need to carry him up and down the stairs until we made other arrangements. Caitlin and I had Julian's room, and my old bedroom was now Aria's nursery. Our original plan was to put Chukee in an extra bedroom upstairs.

"Winson, Kathleen has a roast in the oven for supper. She and Rhoda are fixing everything else. Let me feed Aria and put her down for a nap. You see if Chukee needs anything. We'll set an extra place for him at the table."

"I'm so grateful you have it all together. When I first saw Chukee, I almost didn't recognize him because he's so emaciated. He may be more than we can handle."

"We'll get through this." She put her arm around me and kissed my cheek.

"It's more than just Chukee. Mother is on her way to Vancouver and maybe Lijuan too. I've ached for their safety, and now my desire to bring them here may be fulfilled."

She took hold of my arms and said, "Oh, Winson, that's wonderful. When? How?"

"Eng said Mother's being put on a ship to Vancouver. I don't know when she's arriving. Freeing Lijuan has been more difficult, but hopefully she'll be on a ship soon."

"One day at a time."

"I can't tell you how much I love you. You're an amazing woman."

"And you're pretty amazing yourself. Now see if Chukee needs anything while I take care of Aria."

When Caitlin left the room with Aria, I took Chukee into the bathroom and tended to his toiletry needs, and it reminded me of what I did for Julian. By the time we came out, Aria was sleeping and Sunday dinner was on the table. Chukee's eyes were like saucers as I introduced him to everyone. Rhoda fussed over him and sat next to him at the table. We were all surprised by how much he ate once Rhoda gave him chopsticks.

Chukee said he was tired when dinner was over, so I carried him upstairs and settled him in the extra bedroom. Chukee was now my responsibility. And Caitlin's. Our life had changed in an instant.

My body felt like a string pulled to its limit, and my stomach was in knots, but I wasn't going to break. I needed to be strong for Caitlin and Aria.

Rhoda stood in the doorway. She had carried Chukee's suitcases upstairs and asked if she could help with his meds. I opened the suitcase with his medicine and instructions written in Mandarin. When she offered to administer his injection, I said, "Rhoda, you're an angel."

"You're not going to be able to take care of him here long-term. He must be on the first floor unless you want to install an elevator. My house has a guest bedroom downstairs, and I can take care of him. Since my husband passed, I have too much time on my hands."

"I can't ask that of you, Rhoda. You deserve more of a life than caring for a disabled person."

"I miss caring for someone, and I like Chukee. You've seen what I did for Julian and my husband. You're not asking. I'm offering."

"Thank you for your offer. Let me discuss it with Caitlin."

She put her hands on her hips, widened her stance, narrowed her eyes at me, and said loudly, "Good. In the meantime, I'll come over every day when you're at work and help Caitlin with him. Chukee is too much for Caitlin, so you have no say in how I work this out."

Chukee and Aria slept for a couple of hours, and I had time alone with Caitlin in my office.

"I'm worried about you caring for Aria and Chukee when I'm not home. It's asking too much of you. I know Kathleen can help, but I don't want either of you to deal with Chukee's personal needs, bathe him, or take him to the loo. I'm willing to hire outside assistance, but Rhoda insists on helping and is going to come over every day."

"I'll definitely need her help and am grateful she's willing. Rhoda has a servant's heart and immediately took a liking to Chukee."

"She enjoys caring for people; her life has never been about herself but about doing for others. You know how she sends extra money to her family in the Philippines. Look how long she cared for Julian and her husband. She's certainly strong enough to lift Chukee. She put Chukee to bed and even gave him his shot. Apparently, he has rheumatoid arthritis and is in terrible pain without his medication." I paused for a few moments before I said, "There's this though: his medication is in a clear bottle without a label, so I don't know if it's a prescribed medication or maybe opium. You know this is a criminal gang."

Caitlin's expression changed almost instantly and her eyes widened as she said, "Winson, I simply won't have illegal drugs in this house."

"There are other issues needing legal consideration. We don't have any papers for Chukee or even know his real name. Also, I'm once again in possession of Dung's illegal money. I haven't counted it yet, but there's supposed to be $50,000 in that briefcase." I pointed to the case on the floor next to my desk. "Despite Dung's death, whether his passing is true or not, there's a warrant out for his arrest, an ongoing RCMP investigation, and searches to shutter his operations."

"What have we gotten ourselves into?" She paused until I looked at her, then she said, "Are you going to call Clive?"

"Yes, and also Miss Jerome because Mother and Lijuan will enter Canada illegally."

"Will Eng bring them to Collingwood?"

"No. When the ship comes into Vancouver, they'll be taken to an island off the coast."

"Island! What island? I don't want you to go offshore to an island. Why can't Eng deliver them here like he did Chukee?"

"Eng has a new boss and no longer has Dung's protection. He's also under intense scrutiny from the RCMP."

"After what I went through on Pine Isle, I'm afraid if you go to an unknown island we might never see you again, and that's more than I can handle." Her voice trembled and her face flushed with anger.

I didn't want to put her through any more anxiety. But this was my mother and sister. As we looked into each other's eyes, there was a long silence, and I was hesitant to say something I would regret.

Caitlin was the first to speak. "I know this is your family, and you want to go. But you're my anchor, and I don't want to lose you. And Aria needs her Daddy!"

"I understand your feelings. And, believe me, I don't want to put my life in danger. You and Aria are my world."

"I'm sorry, but you must find another way without going to a remote island. After I was kidnapped, blindfolded, and thinking I'd never see you again and that I'd lose my child, I don't want you or me to relive those circumstances again. And you being out on an island, no, absolutely no!"

Looking at Caitlin, I bit my lip, and acid burned my throat. This was my mother and sister, but Caitlin was the love of my life, and I couldn't put her through another traumatic ordeal. "I promise I won't go to an island alone. I'll speak to Clive to get his thoughts."

"Should you count the money first?"

I nodded, and she watched as I counted the cash. "$25,000, not the promised $50,000. Was this Dung or Eng shorting us?"

"It doesn't matter. It's still illegal money, and you need to call Clive."

"I need to speak with Chief Kirkpatrick too."

Chapter Three

I checked on Chukee, attended to his physical needs, and while he rested after an exhausting day, I called Clive and his wife Bitsy answered the phone. After exchanging pleasantries, I said, "I don't want to interrupt your Sunday, but I'd like to talk to Clive in person, if he's available?"

"I know you wouldn't call unless it was important. He's helping me clean the attic, and I know he would welcome a diversion. Hold on while I ask him."

She returned to the phone and said, "Clive said to come to our house in an hour. That'll give him time to clean up."

Clive answered the door wearing a warm-up suit. "Thanks for getting me out of the attic. Bitsy made us tea and shortbread."

Bitsy greeted me in the kitchen, poured two cups of tea, and excused herself.

"Tell me what's happening."

I told him about Dung's letter, his proposal that if I took care of his invalid brother, Chukee, he would find and bring my mother and sister to Canada and pay me $50,000 for Chukee's care.

He narrowed his eyes and thought for a long moment. "This all happened today?"

"Not exactly. Eng brought me a letter from Dung a few weeks ago, asking if I would care for Chukee, and I asked him to return the next morning for my answer, but he didn't. Apparently, Dung died in the last few days, and that's why Eng delivered Chukee today."

"I assume you know Chukee from the logging camp."

"He liked me because I was kind to him, whereas Dung's thugs ignored him."

"So what's the problem?"

I reviewed with Clive my concerns about Chukee's illegal immigration, contraband medication, and the $25,000 in cash.

"I thought you said $50,000."

"That's what was in Dung's letter but not what's in the briefcase."

Clive's eyebrows arched. "Well, it's dirty money. Have you proof Dung is dead?"

"Eng said he died, but I have no verification. Even if he's dead, his network continues operating, and the RCMP still wants to shut them down."

Clive leaned back in the chair, rubbed his chin, and after a few moments of silence, said, "Except for attorney-client privilege, I would have to disclose what you've told me to the authorities."

"I understand."

"I don't need to remind you that Miss Jerome appointed you to an Immigration Committee authorized by Parliament."

"I plan to call Miss Jerome and Chief Kirkpatrick. I don't want to do anything illegal, but I can be reunited with my mother and sister."

"Is there a reasonable chance Dung has found them?"

"Eng said Mother's on the way to Vancouver, but extracting my sister is problematic. There's another issue, I'm supposed to pick Mother up on an island off the coast, and Caitlin's in a panic over my going. But this involves my mother, how can I not go?"

He rose from the table, paced the room a few times, then stood next me with' his hand on my shoulder, and said, "As your attorney, I can't tell you to do something illegal, but if it was me and there was any chance to save my mother, I would seize the opportunity and figure out how to handle the cash, deal with the Crown, and accommodate my wife's concern."

"How do I accomplish all that?"

He started pacing again as if it helped formulate his thoughts. "I suggest we call Miss Jerome, but off the record. Of course, we'll be taking a chance on how she'll view such disclosures because of her position and your serving on a Parliamentary committee, but not being forthright will bear on your conscience and could have more serious consequences."

"I want to provide full disclosure and do the right thing."

"Come to my office in the morning, and we'll call her together."

"Let's also call Chief Kirkpatrick. I want to be honest with him too."

Bitsy entered the kitchen and said, "Clive, didn't you serve Winson any shortbread?" He pulled back his chair and said, "Sorry love, we were preoccupied."

She rolled her eyes at him. "Sit back down and I'll serve you."

"Bitsy, what's new with you?" I asked.

"I'm working again. Another psychologist referred a war veteran who suffered from a trauma she couldn't help. It's been called 'battle fatigue' and 'shell shock,' among other things. For years, I counseled ex-military who fought during World War II."

"Bitsy, tell him about those you treated while I pour you a cup of tea." He pulled out the chair for her and kissed her cheek.

"I can't reveal confidential patient information, but I can give you an outline of what happened. In 1941, the Canadian Government sent two infantry battalions and a brigade to reinforce British, Indian, and Chinese troops in Hong Kong. They arrived, but without all of their equipment. Then, following the Japanese attack on Pearl Harbor in December, the Japanese attacked Hong Kong with a force four times larger than the Allied troops. Canadian soldiers were asked to counterattack, and after vicious fighting, all the allied forces surrendered and became Japanese war prisoners. I treated Canadian survivors of prison camps for their traumatic neurosis and mental disorders."

"My father fought the Japanese. Mother said he wasn't the same person after the war, and he refused to talk about his time in the military."

"It's likely he suffered from war-related trauma."

Clive poured us tea and took three shortbread from the plate for himself.

"Clive, you know what the doctor said about your diabetes," Bitsy said.

"But you baked the cookies, which you know I can't resist."

When he frowned at her, she added, "You're right, so I'd better stop baking." She smiled at me, then looked directly at Clive and said, "I'm sending all the cookies home with Winson." Turning to me, she asked, "How are Caitlin and Aria?"

"Terrific. Caitlin and I enjoy being parents. Aria is a blessing, especially since she's finally sleeping through the night."

"I imagine she's changed plenty since I last saw her."

"I can't believe how much she's grown. She rolls over and can almost sit by herself. She mimics the sounds she hears, in fact, she's jabbering all the time. It sounds like she's saying DaDa, but that's what I want to hear."

"I'll come by and see her soon."

As I was leaving, Bitsy gave me a bag of shortbread and said, "Kiss beautiful little Aria for me."

~

Clive and I called Miss Jerome Monday morning, and after I described my turn of events, she said, "Dung is wanted and leader of a large crime syndicate under investigation. If he's dead and someone else has taken over, we must find and stop them. I empathize with your mother and sister's situation, and it's noble you're caring for Dung's disabled brother, but because of Dung and the syndicate, I must report what I hear."

"Would it be possible to grant my mother and sister political asylum? If they're sent back to China, they'll be killed. I can still help bring down the syndicate."

"Given your circumstances, I want to give the situation more thought. Call me tomorrow afternoon at four o'clock."

We called Chief Kirkpatrick and appraised him of the situation and our call with Miss Jerome. He said he would await her response.

We called her the next day, exchanged pleasantries, and then she said, "After reflecting on your circumstances, I had a heavy heart and couldn't sleep wondering what I would do in your situation. Unfortunately, I have no choice but to report what you told me about Dung to the RCMP. They may want to take Chukee into custody to force Dung or Eng to come out into the open."

"Chukee won't be of any help to the authorities. The new syndicate boss doesn't care about him and Eng doesn't have enough authority. Chukee's an innocent victim of his brother's occupation. Where does that leave my mother and sister?"

"I'll schedule a meeting for you with David Yonge, an immigration attorney in Vancouver, to discuss establishing legal citizenship for them. He'll do his best to keep them from being returned to China."

"What about the money?"

"Don't spend it yet. If you're allowed to keep Chukee, you'll need the money for his care. I understand you're in a difficult situation, but this is the best I can do for you today. Maybe the situation will change after I contact the RCMP."

After the call, I was concerned but hopeful and updated Chief Kirkpatrick. Three days later, Miss Jerome's secretary called and said Yonge would be attending a two-day planning meeting at the end of next week in Ottawa, and Miss Jerome set up a Saturday morning meeting for Yonge to meet me privately at her home. I agreed and made arrangements to take a train to Ottawa on Friday. The secretary called back and said Miss Jerome reserved a room in my name at the Chateau Laurier. Caitlin and I stayed there on our last visit to Ottawa. It's a beautiful hotel, but our stay was difficult because of altercations with Tak.

While preparing for the train to Ottawa, Caitlin said she'd put extra money in my wallet in case I needed it. Kathleen watched Aria while Caitlin drove me to the train station and prayed for me. I know she had nightmares over our last trip to Ottawa.

I was leaving Chukee with Caitlin and didn't want her, Rhoda, or Kathleen to try to lift him. Thankfully, Kai agreed to carry him upstairs at night and downstairs in the morning. We set up a recliner for him in the parlor, where he could see Aria in her playpen. She would jabber at him, and he would point and giggle at her. Being around a baby was a new experience, but he delighted in her.

When the train passed through the countryside, the natural beauty brought back memories from our previous trip. I went to the dining car for dinner and was reading the newspaper when the waiter approached my table. "Excuse me, Sir, I've waited on you before and taken food back to the baggage car at your request."

"Washington, I remember you. It's good to see you."

His face lit up. "Thank you, Sir, for remembering my name."

"I recall we talked about Ray Morris. Is he still working on the train?"

"No, Sir. Mr. Morris is an important man now, our Union President. He works to provide benefits for all of us porters. And look here, Wash is on my name tag." He held up his name tag for me to see with a big grin.

"His becoming Union President is great news. Please tell Ray hello for me when you see him."

"Thank you, Sir. May I suggest the Chicken Cordon Bleu for dinner."

"As long as you bring an extra serving for me to send to the baggage car, if you're carrying extra cargo."

"Thank you, Sir. We do have extra cargo on this trip," he said with a wink.

Ray Morris had brought food back to Jackson, Kai, and me when we were riding in the baggage car after we escaped from Dung's camp. I still remember this tall, lanky, imposing man with a lean face and expressive eyes. He told us about working conditions for a porter on the train cleaning cars and serving passengers with no place to take a break and eating leftover food from the passengers' plates. The porters weren't called by their names but by 'Boy' or 'George' or 'Hey George,' after the sleeping car's inventor, George Pullman.

When Wash served dinner, I asked, "I hope Ray's been able to improve your working conditions."

"After we unionized, Ray negotiated an agreement with Pullman, and we received pay increases, paid vacation, overtime, our own regular meals, and a small space on the train to eat and sleep."

"I'm glad for you, Wash."

Toward the end of dinner, I opened my wallet and was shocked to see several hundred dollars, courtesy of Caitlin. I left Wash a generous tip and a note telling him I was paying for extra food to be delivered to the baggage car.

∽

Upon arrival at the train station, I walked on the platform and looked at where Caitlin and I had stood when Tak attacked us. I said a silent prayer, then walked to the Chateau Laurier Hotel. William, the bellman, greeted me as I approached the entrance. "Mr. LeBlanc, it's a pleasure to have you staying with us again. Let me tend to your bag. Will Mrs. LeBlanc be joining you?"

"William, you make me feel welcomed, as you did on my last visit. This trip, my wife is home with our newborn daughter, Catherine Aria."

"What a great name. How old is she?"

"Six months."

"I hope to see them both staying with us soon."

"Aria would love all the lights."

"The hotel is ornately decorated in winter, and the city is magical this time of year."

"Thank you, William. Maybe next winter when she's old enough to enjoy the snow."

I checked into the hotel, freshened up in the room, and decided to stretch my legs. I walked to Parliament Hill and around the grounds and contemplated all the events that occurred on the previous trip to Ottawa. The stars were out, and there was a light dusting of snow on the grass, but nothing to prevent a vigorous walk. It was almost midnight when I turned in for the night.

I took a cab to Miss Jerome's home in the Sandy Hill neighborhood on Saturday morning. Her home was two stories with red brick, a wood shake roof, and located on a quiet cul-de-sac. The entrance was through a small private courtyard.

Miss Jerome welcomed me and asked me to call her Ellen while in her home. Once inside the entrance hall, the main living area was a few steps lower and featured floor to ceiling windows overlooking the river a few hundred feet below. A river-stone fireplace was to my left and a dining room to the right where David Yonge stood to greet me.

"Winson, let me introduce you to the Honourable Parliament Member David Yonge."

I extended my hand, and he took it in both hands with the warmest smile and said, "It's a pleasure to meet another Chinese professional in Canada. Please call me David."

"The pleasure's all mine. I've been fortunate."

"I've had good fortune come my way too."

David was over six feet tall, trim and athletic, with dashing good looks, chiseled facial features, a sophisticated charm, and graceful movements. I read that he was the first Chinese Member of Parliament, which was quite an accomplishment.

While her maid served us tea, Miss Jerome said, "You're both humble men. I know you're hard workers and have taken the high ground of just action."

"I was surprised to learn a Chinese man had been elected to Parliament."

"We're making good strides in this country to stop discrimination, thanks to the efforts of Ellen and other MPS's, but it still exists."

"David was the first Chinese Canadian to be accepted to the British Columbia bar, the first to appear before the B.C. Court of Appeals, and the first to be elected to Parliament. In 1944, when Canada considered the Chinese to be less than full citizens, he risked his life by volunteering for duty as a saboteur and spy behind Japanese lines. After the war and as a veteran, he finally earned citizenship and the right to vote. He campaigned to redress wrongs committed against fellow Chinese Canadians. His ambition has been to convince Canadian society to dismantle legally sanctioned racism."

Ellen looked at David and said, "I applaud David's work and am trying to emulate him in my efforts to seek equal rights for women."

Ellen provided background on her history with me and made a point to mention my marriage to Caitlin and our young daughter. Then, she asked me, "Please tell David about your Chinese family's situation."

"I'm sure Ellen has told you I came to Canada illegally but didn't know it at the time. My parents thought they were sending me to a sponsoring family, but it was human trafficking, and I was fortunate to get out. Sometime later, I was sponsored and adopted by a banker in Collingwood named Julian LeBlanc, who provided my legal citizenship. I've been in Canada eighteen years and left behind my mother, father, grandfather, and sister."

"And your mother and sister are on their way to Canada and desire citizenship."

"My mother is currently en route to Vancouver by ship. My sister's passage has not been confirmed."

"Tell me about them."

"My mother, Lil, was university educated and taught the equivalent of high school science in Hangzhou. After I left, she was removed from her classroom by the Red Guard and deported to a mountain region to teach peasants. My sister, Lijuan, was twelve when I left home, and was forced into the service of General Lin Biao to be his concubine."

"Ellen didn't say much about how your mother and sister were rescued from China."

"Winson, before you go any further, there are complications I can't be involved with, so I suggest you hire David to represent you, your mother, and your sister," Ellen interjected.

"Give me one dollar for a retainer, then we can talk, and everything you tell me will remain confidential," David said.

"I'll leave the two of you to discuss matters and will be in my office if you need me," Ellen said, excusing herself from the conversation.

When I gave David a dollar, he smiled and said, "Now, tell me more about the circumstances around bringing your family to Canada."

"I'm sure Ellen told you about Dung and the syndicate he headed."

"She did, and I'm aware that he's wanted by federal and provincial authorities."

"I've been told he's dead, but he had connections in China, I don't know who or how, but he arranged passage for my mother and sister on separate ships to Vancouver, but they'll be arriving without proper papers. Is there any way to bring them in legally? Or could they possibly receive political asylum?"

"Do you know what ships they're arriving on?"

"I won't be notified until after their arrival."

"Since they're already en route, and we don't know the ships or their arrival dates, we can't meet them at the pier and grant them political asylum. Fortunately, we can submit applications in advance to process their entry under the "Chinese Adjustment Statement Program."

"I appreciate whatever you can do to help facilitate their immigration. I'd like them to arrive legally and am concerned about picking them up on an unknown island. My wife doesn't want me to go. She was abducted while vacationing with a friend on an island about a year ago and still has nightmares."

"I don't blame her and agree it wouldn't be a good idea for you to go to an island. Maybe you can negotiate to bring them to Chinatown in Vancouver, and I could be with you to meet them. I have an office and apartment near Chinatown. If you want to stay with me, my home is yours."

"That's kind of you. I don't want to put anyone else in harm's way. These are extremely dangerous people."

"Dangerous people, whom the government wants to stop. After your family is safe, we'll need your help to bring them down."

"I'm willing to cooperate. Dung was the leader, but a new boss took over upon his death, and I don't know his name. My contact is Eng, a former guard at the logging camp, now the head of the southern operation."

"Do you know how to contact Eng?"

"No, but I suspect he's operating offshore."

"Let's get the paperwork started for your mother and sister; then all we can do is wait for you to hear from Eng."

We said our goodbyes to Ellen, and he offered to drive me back to the hotel. On the way, he said, "I came into a windfall from a new client this morning and will treat you to lunch at my favorite restaurant where you can order Szechuan or Cantonese." His laugh was contagious.

"There are no good Chinese restaurants in Collingwood."

"The Cathay Inn is a popular spot for politicians to frequent. I know the owner and his father so I eat there whenever I'm in town. The father opened his first restaurant in Vancouver's Chinatown in the 1920s. Both are successful restaurants."

"This doesn't look like Vancouver's Chinatown."

"It started with three grocery stores, two laundries, two recreation clubs, and one gift shop and grew after the war but then declined because it was near Ottawa's town center, and the old buildings were gradually replaced by high-rise offices."

We entered the Cathay Inn through bright red doors with brass lion-head door knockers and ornamental studs. David said the number of studs represented the status of the owner. We were greeted in Mandarin by the host and sat at a corner table. The decorations, smells, and food reminded me of Hangzhou. During lunch, he told me he was born in Victoria in 1924, and his father was an immigrant from Guangdong Province. He grew up in a world where property covenants forbade Chinese from buying land in many neighborhoods and were barred from the practice of pharmacy, medicine, and the law.

"How did you become a lawyer?"

"I joined the military. The British wanted to recruit soldiers of Chinese background who could be sent into Asian jungles to blend in with the local population as secret agents. When the Canadian government reversed a policy barring Chinese immigrants from serving in the armed forces, I enlisted and volunteered for clandestine warfare. Our Chinese troop organized resistance behind Japanese lines in Borneo. We looked like mercenaries because we didn't wear military uniforms and were unshaven. All of us were prepared to put our lives on the line with no guarantee the Canadian government would give us the full rights of Canadian citizenship. We took a gamble, and after my service, I took advantage of veterans' benefits to complete a Bachelor of Arts and a law degree at the University of British Columbia. In 1947, the provincial government ended restrictions on voting for Chinese Canadians, and the federal government revoked its discriminatory immigration laws. In the end, the Chinese veterans were appreciated and allowed citizenship."

"That's amazing. And from practicing law, you entered politics."

"Well, not right away. I practiced law for several years and ran for Parliament in 1956 and lost. Two years later, I ran again and won but not without difficulties."

"I imagine you faced prejudices and struggles. Are you married?"

"Divorced. I was married to a Canadian woman for a few years but many things went wrong."

"I'm sorry to hear. My wife is an Irish Canadian from Ontario, and we've been married for three years. We just had our first child, Catherine Aria, but we call her Aria. I feel blessed, but we've faced a good deal of adversity."

"How did you meet your wife?"

I told him how we met, fell in love, and the difficulties we faced with the reaction from her parents and friends, including what Kathleen's husband tried to do.

"Maybe I need to engage you in advising me on inter-racial relationships, and in exchange, I'll provide my immigration services. It could be a reciprocal consulting arrangement."

"You're selling yourself short."'

"Well, you don't know how much help I'll need, so you may end up with the short stick."

He extended his hand across the table, and a warm smile lit up his face. When I took his hand, he said, "I want to know everything. Your history, how you came to Canada, your family situation, and how you got the leader of a major crime ring to bring your family out of Mao-controlled China, anything you might have left out so far."

"Whenever you have time."

"How about now. The owner won't mind, and if you're staying over, we can meet again tomorrow."

"I would like that." I sensed his compassion and understanding.

For the next several hours, I told him my story. Then we discussed Dung's proposal and my custody of Chukee.

After hearing my story, David said, "And I thought I lived an eventful life."

During our meal, I noticed the busboy servicing our table. He looked familiar, and I tried to engage him, but he shied away from looking at me even when I spoke directly to him in Mandarin.

Something about him kept pricking my memory. I knew him from somewhere. While we were waiting for the check, he was standing unoccupied at a waiter serving table. I excused myself and walked over to him.

He wouldn't make eye contact with me.

"You look familiar. Do we know each other?" I asked.

He kept his head down and shrugged his shoulders.

"I feel like I've seen you before. Where are you from?"

"Hangzhou." His voice was so soft I strained to hear.

"I came from Hangzhou as well, on the *Pacific Northwest Steamship* on my way to a sponsoring Chinese family, but I was made a slave in a logging camp."

"Yes, I know."

I peered at his gaunt, hardened face, and when we made eye contact, he said, "You are Tao Wen Shun, and I was on the ship with you."

"Chun!" He was bright and robust on the ship, but in Dung's camp, he was tortured until he broke. After our first attempt to escape the camp, Chun was in the cell next to Kai and told him how Dung paid off the RCMP officers in return for not reporting his illegal activities. I touched his arm and said, "My friend, it's good to see you."

He stepped back, and his dark eyes darted around as he said, "Please, not here."

I looked at the customers in the dining room and said, "I don't care what others may think."

"Sir, please. It is not the diners that concern me."

"Chun, what happened to you since the logging camp?"

He fidgeted and said in a hushed tone, "I was sold from one crime ring to another and am being leased to this restaurant. I still have debt to pay."

"How much do you owe?"

"I will never have..."

He stopped abruptly as a waiter approached and said, "Sir, do you need something?"

"Thank you, but I was talking to this young man."

The waiter looked sternly at Chun and said, "Make it quick. He has work to do."

When the waiter walked away I asked, "Can we go outside to talk?"

"I am not allowed to speak to customers. Please go to your table," and he walked away.

When I returned to the table, David asked, "What was that about?"

"That young man was a prisoner in the logging camp with me and is still indentured."

"To this restaurant! The owner's a friend and has plenty of explaining to do. If he were here today, I would confront him. There's more than one reason why we've met."

"On the way out, I'll slip Chun cash and my business card and put a note on the back to please call so I can help him get his life back."

"Give him my card too, and tell him I'll process his paperwork for free."

"I could have been Chun, except for a guiding hand that changed my fate."

When I handed Chun our cards and cash, he choked back his emotions and bowed his head.

David drove me back to my hotel, and we set a time to meet in the morning. Although we'd only known each other one day, I felt a brotherly affinity for David. Our journeys, although different, had similarities, including marrying into a different race. He was warm and caring, but there was sadness when he spoke of his marriage.

When I called Caitlin, she said, "Love, I had my hand on the phone to call you."

After hearing how everything was at home, I told her about meeting David and his willingness to help get Mother and Lijuan legal citizenship. "David said he'd like to meet you."

"Invite him to visit us. We always have room for a friend."

"Now you're joking. We already have a full house with Kathleen and Chukee, and soon Mother and Lijuan will arrive."

"The more, the merrier."

❧

It was six-thirty in the morning when the phone rang. Caitlin's voice cracked as she spoke. "Love, Daddy's gone. He didn't wake up this morning."

"I'm so sorry. Are you with your Mother?"

"No, I'm going to see her now. Kathleen's here to watch Aria and will call Rhoda to come early."

"I'll be on the next train home."

"There's nothing you can do."

"I can be there for you and take care of things at home so you can spend time with your mother. Had your father complained about feeling ill?"

"Mum said he had indigestion the last few days. She suggested he see the doctor, but you know Daddy."

"He was a force of nature."

"But he was softening. A few days ago, he even told me you were a good husband and father. He loved Aria and enjoyed being a grandfather."

Caitlin was silent for a few moments, then said, "Daddy was impossible. He couldn't sit still, except when he slept, but Mom said even then, he constantly tossed and turned and never seemed to settle."

"When did you see him last?"

"A week ago, I met him at the pub for lunch. He said things to me that day which made me feel whole with him again. About how he loved who I had grown up to be, even when I stood up to him. I took Aria with me, and he held her the whole time."

"Oh my, love, what a special conversation. Why didn't you tell me when it happened?"

"I try not to mention my father to you. It keeps things simpler between us. I wish I could see Daddy again and talk like we did that day. I don't think I'll ever go back to that pub."

"Yes, you can, with me. I'm sorry he won't be able to see his granddaughter grow up. How's your mum?"

"She's tough. She had to be, married to Daddy. They were together for over forty years."

"If you want her to stay with us, it's good with me."

"Our angel's awake and wants my attention. I'll take her with me to Mum's. I love you, Winson LeBlanc."

After the call, I reflected on my relationship with Kierian and had mixed feelings. I tried to be a good son-in-law. He'd be nice to me for a while but then say something cruel. A few weeks ago, Maureen called him a jerk when he remarked about the shape of Aria's eyes and hoped they wouldn't become slanted. I hurt for Caitlin but wouldn't miss the conflict.

～∽～

Before checking out of the hotel, I called David Yonge and told him about Caitlin's father, apologized for canceling our meeting, then invited him to stay with us for a weekend.

So much good had happened in Ottawa. We had a plan for legalizing immigration for my mother and sister, and I met Chun and hoped he would contact me for help to become a legal citizen with David's help.

～∽～

The funeral took place on Thursday and was attended by many of her parent's friends. Aria was an angel and slept in my arms through most of the service. As we walked to the reception hall, Caitlin held my arm and whispered, "I was about to lose it at the funeral. I'm so glad you're here for me."

"I'll always be here for you. This is going to be a difficult time for your mother. You'll need to be there for her."

"Kathleen offered to stay with her for a while. Rhoda is at the house every day to help with Chukee, and I can take care of Aria. I've appreciated your letting Kathleen live with us so long."

"She's family. Our home is her home."

At the reception, I walked around with Aria, praying it would be a healing time for Caitlin and her mother while they met with their friends in a long receiving line; then Maureen took Aria to show her off.

A few minutes later, Caitlin walked up and took my hand. "You're amazing with Aria. She missed her long nap, but she hasn't fussed at all."

"It's easy when she sleeps in my arms. Look at your mum. She's glowing, carrying Aria around to her friends."

"Mum loves being a grandmother, and Daddy loved being a grandfather. He said something else I didn't share with you. He thought you were incredible to overlook how he treated you. He said without your help, his reputation wouldn't have been restored, and he'd still be blamed for the Montebello accident. You gave him dignity again."

"You're the one who asked me to overlook his behavior and help him. I did it because I love you."

"Mum has always liked and defended you but she couldn't change or challenge Daddy." She sniffled. "I love you for who you are, and I love you for the way you love me."

"I do love you, my beautiful wife and mother of our adorable daughter," I said as I put my arm around her waist, pulled her toward me, and kissed her cheek. "And Maureen has been the best mother-in-law I could ask for."

Life was temporary, but my love for Caitlin and Aria was forever. They completed my life.

Two weeks after the burial, I went to the grave, took a picture of Kierian holding Aria, and laid it among the dried flowers. I placed a stone on the grave, like I did for Julian and Jackson, praying that God would keep his departed soul in His hand, as a shepherd would keep a stone in his sling to protect his flock, and bid him farewell.

I was glad to hear that his conscience had awakened in his recent talks with Caitlin. Who are we without reflection and a sense of right and wrong?

That night in bed, I thought about losing someone we love, it makes us feel sad, but then we find an outlet for that loss. For Maureen, it would be Caitlin and Aria, and for Caitlin, it would be Aria and me. I was blessed to be married to a strong woman with a good heart.

I inhaled deeply, filled with the scent of my beautiful wife, and fell sound asleep with my arms around her.

Chapter Four

Monday morning at the bank, I received a phone call from Eng.

"Your mother arrived, and we have her on the island. When can you pick her up?"

"It'll take me at least three days on the train."

"Can you fly?"

"I'll see if I can get a flight out of Toronto. Can I call you back?"

"I'll call you in three hours."

I had more questions than answers, and my life continued to be in turmoil. The situation at home would be drastically different with Mother in the house, but maybe Mother would be a help for Chukee since they both speak Mandarin.

My first call was to Caitlin. When I told her about Mother, she said, "You better not go to any island."

"David Yonge is there to help me. I'll try to get a flight later today or tomorrow morning."

"I'm unhappy about this, but I'll drive you to Toronto."

"Mother's never been on a plane, and I don't know her condition, so I'll bring her home on the train. It'll give me time with her. I know this is difficult for you, but I promise to be careful."

When I called Clive, he said he'd have one of his assistants research the islands off the coast of Vancouver and try to have information for me before I had to meet Eng.

Later in the afternoon, Matthew Baine, a paralegal in Clive's office, walked into the bank, dropped several books, a file, and maps on my desk, and said, "Mr. LeBlanc, I may have found your island. There was an outbreak of leprosy in Vancouver near the turn of the century, and five unfortunate Chinese men were found riddled with it in the damp back alleys of Chinatown. Public officials acted quickly to get the Province's approval to transfer them to D'Arcy Island. It was a leprosy colony from 1891 to 1924, and when it was finally abandoned, bootleggers used it as a staging area to illegally import liquor into the United States."

"Could D'Arcy be where my mother is?"

He opened a map and pointed to a small island between Vancouver Island and the mainland in the shipping channel.

"It looks like ocean-going vessels would go right by the island. It would be a good place to drop contraband," he said.

"In this situation, humans are the contraband."

"Current records show it's uninhabited and appears to be owned by the Province."

⁂

I drove home after work, parked in the garage, and entered the back door. Maureen and Kathleen were preparing dinner. We usually ate in the kitchen, but the table wasn't set. Kathleen said, "Kai came over a little while ago to help Rhoda take Chukee upstairs. Chukee had a bad day, and Rhoda thought it best for him to be in bed. Caitlin invited Kai and Wei Lei back for dinner."

I kept thinking about Mother, Eng, and the trip. The last thing I wanted was to entertain people, and I was upset with Caitlin for having a dinner party when she walked in with Aria in her arms, who let out a joyful squeal and reached for me.

"Your girls have been waiting for you," Caitlin said with a smile.

"Leave me alone for a while," I looked at Caitlin with tears welling in my eyes and went to my office to hide my anxiety. I closed the door, poured myself a Scotch, and sat at my desk. I could feel anger boiling, but I didn't need to take it out on Caitlin and Aria. I had almost finished my drink when Caitlin knocked on the door and walked in without Aria.

"We need to talk. Why are you angry with me? What have I done?"

"This house is like the Hangzhou train station, people always coming and going, never any peace and quiet, and it's only going to get worse. I'm not ready for this and have no choice but to pick up my mother."

"Did you speak to David?"

"He's meeting me at the airport, and I've booked a room at the Vancouver Hotel. It's near the train station, and Eng is supposed to contact me at about three o'clock tomorrow afternoon. I told him I wanted to pick up Mother in Vancouver, but he won't have an answer until tomorrow."

"Don't meet Eng by yourself. I don't trust them?"

"The lives of my mother and sister are at stake so I need to cooperate. This situation is overwhelming, and I still have a bank to run. I wish you hadn't invited company for dinner."

"Kai wants to go with you for protection."

"That's kind of him. I'll take a quick shower and be ready for company."

At dinner, when Kai said he wanted to go with me, Wei Lei shouted, "You want to head back to hell, to the trafficking ring, to a place you never wanted to even think about again, and to the gangsters you've been running away from. They are why we moved to Timmins." Her anger turned to tears, and she said, "You can't go."

"Wife, why not?"

"Are you dense?"

"I'm going to protect my brother. Why are you being so dramatic?"

"Because of our child?" she yelled in Mandarin.

He looked dumbfounded and finally muttered, "Child. What child?"

"Our child. I'm pregnant."

Kai looked at her like he didn't understand, and she repeated, "I'm pregnant."

Without understanding Mandarin, Caitlin and Kathleen immediately and instinctively knew what she had said. Women amazed me with their ability to communicate almost from osmosis. Wei Lei walked to the kitchen, and Maureen, Kathleen, and Caitlin followed her, leaving Kai and me alone.

Kai looked at me and said, "I guess we're finished with dinner."

"You'd better check on your wife."

"She's got plenty of company," Kai said, shaking his head.

"Then, come with me while I check on Chukee. I want to see what he knows about this island Eng mentioned."

Chukee was awake when we opened the door. "Cauliflower, you still here?"

Kai rubbed his ear. Tak cut off a piece of his ear in the logging camp, trying to force him to tell them where we hid the money from our shoe sales.

"Chukee, do you know the island where your brother took you?"

"Boat ride to island, far away," he replied.

"Do you know the island's name or where it is?"

"Why?"

"I'm supposed to go there to meet my mother. She's coming from China."

"Eng tell you?"

"No. Eng did not tell me."

"Sorry, can't help you find island."

"Have you heard the name D'Arcy Island?"

"Don't know name of island."

Chukee's first loyalty would be to his brother and Eng. I sat with Kai in the parlor, and we talked about Chukee and how Dung cared for him. As we spoke, Kai kept tapping his feet on the hardwood floor.

"Are you nervous?"

"I'm becoming a father. Our lives have been unstable since we've been married. We've struggled and never discussed having a family, and now, we're having a baby."

"Having a child is the most important part of our Chinese culture. You'll continue your family's legacy, and it'll extend from China to Canada."

"My parents will never know I married and will never meet my children."

"But you'll know. Focus on your future and providing for your family, and look to find a secure job. Talk to Wei Lei and make her part of the process. Spend time together, start with what you know, and something will materialize."

"You're right. I need to plan for our future."

"Here I am, giving you advice about the future while I'm stressing Caitlin about traveling to the West Coast to get Mother and then Lijuan. Bringing them into our home will certainly disrupt our lives. They don't speak English, and Caitlin doesn't understand Mandarin. I'm asking a great deal from my wife."

"I still want to go with you to protect you in Vancouver."

"You'd better stay home with Wei Lei, or I'll have both Caitlin and Wei Lei upset at me. Besides, I'll have David Yonge with me in Vancouver."

"I'm glad your mother will get to know Aria. You're lucky to even know your family is still alive."

"I'm fortunate but also apprehensive. It's been eighteen years since I've seen them. Will I even recognize Mother? Her arrival will present many challenges."

After everyone left, I apologized to Caitlin for being angry earlier in the evening and for what I was putting her through with Chukee, Mother, and Lijuan. My understanding wife said everyone goes through changes, and we would adjust and do our best.

&

I didn't know what time it was when Caitlin shook me awake. "Winson, wake up. You're having a nightmare. Wake up. You're struggling to say something." She cradled me in her arms, gently rubbed my back, and whispered, "Honey, I'm right here next to you. It's just a dream. Are you okay?"

"I'm not sure."

"Do you want to talk about it?"

"Dung brought Mother and Lijuan to me long enough for me to embrace them. Then he took Lijuan away and said I could only take Mother, but Mother demanded to stay, so my sister could go with me. Dung said he was keeping Lijuan to ensure I took care of Chukee. Lijuan didn't speak and wouldn't look at me. I'm afraid."

"Of what?"

"A premonition. The new syndicate boss keeps them to control me like Dung manipulated everyone."

Caitlin rubbed my back, curled up around me, cradled me like a baby, and whispered, "I'm sorry for your dream, but it was only a dream. I believe in you and know you'll find a safe way to bring your mother and sister home."

"Every time I've had dreams like this, something significant has followed. When Julian hired Wong, I had hope of finding my family but was crushed bit by bit with each letter, and when Wong couldn't continue the search, my hope was gone, and an ache filled my heart. I'm excited and fearful at the same time. I choose to be expectant and optimistic but don't want to be crushed again."

"Love, we'll work this out; we always do."

I couldn't go to sleep and thought about the unintended consequences. Everything was fluid, and I reflected on the many dramatic changes we'd already experienced. At a certain point, I fell asleep from mental exhaustion. When the alarm went off, I was relieved to get up and eager to leave the dream behind.

I put my arms around Caitlin and whispered, "Thank you for watching over me."

"It took my mind off Aria."

"What do you mean?"

"This was my first night without her. When Mum took her home last night, it was difficult for me. I wonder how she'll do this morning without nursing."

"You're a smart and wonderful mother. You had breast milk in the freezer, so she'll do fine until you return home, but we'll stop before we get to the airport and call to check on her."

I affectionately kissed her neck, and she said, "We need to get moving. You have a plane to catch."

We left at five in the morning to drive to Toronto for my flight, and because the flight was so early, Kai came over before we left to stay with Chukee until Rhoda arrived.

My first question to David was, "Have you ever heard of D'Arcy Island?"

"Is that where you think your mother is?"

"I don't know. My attorney in Collingwood did specific research and said it was a place the government sent Chinese people with leprosy."

"That's true, but it's been uninhabited since the last leper died almost fifty years ago."

"Is it close to Vancouver?"

"An hour or so by boat. Let's hope we don't have to go there."

Chapter Five

We drove to the hotel in the pouring rain and were in my room when the phone rang at three o'clock, I answered, and a husky male voice speaking Mandarin said, "There is a package for you in the lobby."

"I'll be there in a few minutes."

"Now!" he shouted, "Or you will be taking a boat ride." Then the phone clicked off.

We rushed out the door and took the stairs as fast as we dared, too excited to wait for the elevator. When I stepped into the lobby, I was shocked to see a large Chinese man wearing a black raincoat too small for his body, and next to him was a diminutive person wearing a black plastic hooded rain jacket, looking at the ground.

"This one for you," he said, pushing the small figure toward me.

The last time I saw my mother, she was a few inches shorter than me, but I could look into her eyes. The woman in front of me barely came to my chest. In Mandarin, I said, "Please look at me."

There was no movement.

"Answer him," the man demanded as he shoved her closer to me.

I looked at the big man, "Don't push her."

His jowls shook as he snorted with irritation.

"Do I know you? Are you Zhang?" Zhang was Dung's feeder agent in Hangzhou.

Standing close to him, I was nauseated by his foul odor. He had put on a few pounds since I last saw him at the Imperial Groceries & General Merchandise store to discuss my sponsorship to Canada, but he still had a mean spirit. Through him, my life pivoted and spun out of control, and my youth was forfeited. With his fleshy hand, he pushed my mother toward me again. There were no gold rings on his massive hands like he wore in Hangzhou. I was full of doubt if this really was my mother.

I gently lifted the woman's chin and struggled to get words out of my mouth. "Mother. Mother?" Did I say them aloud or to myself? I certainly didn't recognize her, and she didn't appear to know me. It wasn't beyond the syndicate's capabilities to pawn off another woman as my mother and try to extort money from me later.

She glanced at me with no change in expression but didn't maintain eye contact.

"If your name is Lil and you were married to Tai in Hangzhou, you're my mother, and I'm Tao Wen Shun, your son."

"You are not my son. He disappeared many years ago."

It'd been more than half my life since I watched her standing on the dock as my ship departed. I yearned to wrap my arms around her but didn't want to frighten her. Was she really my mother, standing before me in a country she adopted ideas from but never expected to see?

My mind played games between what I wanted and what was in front of me; nevertheless, I reached for her arm, and when I touched her, she pulled away.

"Please come with me. You'll be safe."

When I took hold of her arm, she flinched, then looked at Zhang. He pushed her into my chest and said, "Now you belong to him," then turned his back and walked away.

David approached me and put his hand on my shoulder. "She needs time to adjust, so take her to your room, and I'll check on you in a few hours. There's a train at seven o'clock in the morning; I'll make a reservation for a sleeping car. If she needs medical attention, I can call a doctor."

I nodded nervously while I kept my eyes on her. How was I to calm her fears? So much had changed in eighteen years.

"Please believe me when I say I'm your son, and I won't hurt you."

Her body trembled and she squeezed her hands together and chewed on her fingernails.

"I promise I'll give you freedom from those that brought you here."

Her eyes looked in the direction Zhang had left, and then around the lobby. "What is happening? You can't be my son."

"Let me tell you my story."

"Where are we?"

"In a hotel. Come with me so we can talk."

She reluctantly followed me as I walked to the elevator, but when the door opened, and I motioned for her to enter, she stepped back and shook her head. Either she'd never been in an elevator or didn't trust me.

"Let's go to the restaurant for tea and talk."

We sat at a corner table in the dining room, and when I took hold of her plastic covering, she clutched it. "It's wet. Let me remove it."

She didn't look at me as she cautiously released her grip and let me take it off. She wore a tattered but heavy wool coat under the thin layer of plastic, and when I removed it, her army green shirt and pants hung loosely on her frail body. She had always been slim but now was almost emaciated. Her unkempt hair was mostly gray, and she pushed back in the chair. I ordered tea, then said, "I am your son, Tao Wen Shun."

"My son is dead."

This wasn't the reception or conversation I'd envisioned, but then I knew nothing about what she'd been through.

"Please look at me." I lifted my arms wide with my palms open toward her.

Her eyes scanned my face. "The last time I saw my son was..."

"1949. On the pier as I boarded the Pacific Northwest Steamship."

Her eyes widened and she looked like a frightened bird, held her arms close to her body, and rocked back and forth.

"Where am I?"

"Vancouver, Canada."

She hadn't been told she was being taken to her son in Canada.

"Those who took me knew my name. You work with them. Who are you?"

"I don't work for the men who brought you here. I'm Tao Wen Shun, your son." I opened my shirt collar. "I'm still wearing YeYe's pendant. He gave it to me as I boarded the ship to leave you, and I never take it off. This should prove that I am your son."

"No, no. You must have killed my son. Oh, my poor son. You are a monster."

"Mother, I don't know what else to say to convince you." With tears in my eyes, I lifted the pendant over my head. "Here, take your father's medallion."

I held it out for her to take, and when I saw her expression, I was convinced she was my mother.

"You stole it from my son!"

"I'm your son. When I left Hangzhou, you gave me a jade pendant as a gift to give to the mother of my sponsoring family. You told me that jade stands for beauty, grace, and purity."

"How can it be possible that you are my son?"

Her brown eyes darted about the room, and her hands shook as she held the medallion against her chest.

"Do you remember packing a pair of heavy fleece-lined pants for me? You turned one leg inside out to show me the inner pocket you sewed to keep my money safe."

She put her hand to her mouth.

"You and YeYe gave me thirty-five Yuan."

"Only my son would know those things. But it cannot be! It is impossible that you are him!" Her eyes narrowed, and she asked, "What is your brother's name?"

"I have no brother, only a sister named Lijuan. She went with you and Cousin Liu Yang to a fortune teller before I left home."

"What do you remember of my father?"

"My YeYe? He was a master craftsman who made erhus and xiaos. I helped him in his workshop and would go to the docks for snakeskins. I still have the xiao he made, and you painted double happiness on it for me."

She paled as if she had seen a ghost and braced herself against the chair as she looked around the room like a frightened animal, then a shiver coursed through her.

"I'll let you go anytime you want, but what if I am your son?"

She narrowed her eyes.

"You don't know anyone here and can't return to China. Spend time with me, and then you can decide what you want to do."

She took several sips of tea and said, "You will let me go?"

"Yes, and I'll take you wherever you want."

"I will go with you."

"I have a room in this hotel, I will not harm or touch you, but you need to change your wet clothes. Let me introduce you to the front desk, and if you don't want to stay, I'll tell them to help you."

We went to the receptionist, and I introduced her and asked them to give her a key to the room. She reluctantly followed me in the elevator, and when we entered the room, she looked about and focused on the two beds.

"If you want, I'll rent another room, and you can stay here by yourself." Her shoulders dropped. "Please sit, and I'll give you a blanket for warmth."

She avoided the bed and sat in an easy chair. I wrapped a blanket around her shoulders and knelt at her feet, hoping my posture would help her relax and convey my respect and submission.

"Did you come to Canada with my son? Is that how you know so much about him and my family?"

Why wouldn't she accept the fact I was her son? I'd given her plenty of convincing evidence, but she still distrusted me. Her life must have been extremely difficult. She'd been abused by Mao's soldiers and separated from her father, husband, and daughter. In the process, she lost trust in humanity. Her world had fallen apart, and now she distrusted everyone and everything.

"I don't want you to do anything that makes you uncomfortable, but it's been eighteen years since I've been with you. Can I hold your hand?" I didn't know why I asked, but her brown eyes softened.

"You asked those same words when you were little."

The blanket dropped from her shoulders as she took my left hand. Hesitantly, she reached out and took my right hand. Her once creamy smooth skin was thick and rough, her face weathered, and her hands calloused. When I looked into her eyes, they were filled with pain. I wasn't sure if I should speak or be still and hold hands. It was enough to be together.

She cleared her throat, stared at me, and purposefully said, "You are Tao Wen Shun!" When she said those words, she pulled my hands to her mouth and kissed them.

"Tao Wen Shun," she said, shaking her head in disbelief.

I bowed my head before her. She put her hand under my chin, slowly lifted my head, and asked, "Are you an apparition kneeling before me?"

"No. I'm your son, who has always loved you. I've searched many years for you."

Moments went by as she composed herself. Finally, catching her breath, she said, "I cannot believe this is happening. Can it be true you are my son?"

"It's true, and today my deepest longing has been fulfilled."

She covered her eyes and said, "I never expected to see you again. When you boarded the ship and were beyond my vision, I would have given anything for one more day with you. Instead, I have lived for years with a wounded heart."

"Now it can heal. I know the road you walked has been difficult, but you're with me now, and your tormentors are on the other side of the ocean."

"But the beast who brought me to you is here! He did unspeakable things to me, and I cannot bear to look at him."

"We'll be leaving Vancouver tomorrow, leaving Zhang behind. I'm taking you to my home, a three-day journey by train from here, where you'll be far away from Zhang."

"Far way."

She placed her head on my shoulder but did not cry. I held her, closed my eyes, listened to her every breath, and hoped the pain she carried would find release in the days ahead.

"I know you must be exhausted. Let me fill the bathtub for you."

"Is there a bath down the hall?"

"There's a complete bath in this room, bathtub, upright toilet, and sink. There's shampoo and conditioner to wash your hair and a clean robe on the back of the door. Take your time and enjoy the warm water. If you want to be alone, I can wait in the hallway and stand guard. I want you to be comfortable."

"Stay here. I do not want to lose sight of my son!"

While she was in the tub, I called Caitlin, who was relieved my mother was safe and had been delivered to the hotel. I called David to thank him for his help, and he said, "I noticed your mother had no luggage, so I stopped at a store on my way home and picked up a few items for her. They should be delivered to your room shortly."

He was such a thoughtful man. By the time Mother was out of the bathroom, a package had arrived, and when she opened the box, she said, "I cannot accept these."

"This is a gift from the man who was with me downstairs. It would be an insult for you to refuse them."

Inside the box was a coat, two simple dresses, underclothes, a nightgown, a hairbrush, and a toothbrush. "Tell him I am grateful but have no way to repay him."

"It'll please him if you wear these clothes."

"Would you mind if I put on the nightgown? It has been an exciting but exhausting day."

"Of course. I'll order food to be delivered to this room."

"It would be too expensive to order such food."

"I can take care of it. I'll order something light."

"I do not know if I can eat."

When the food arrived, she ate a little soup but had difficulty keeping her eyes open. "You're tired, and we have an early train in the morning and need our sleep. We have three days together before you meet my wife and daughter."

"You are married and have a child?

"My wife is Caitlin, and our daughter, Catherine Aria, is almost seven months old. We call her Aria. I'm glad you'll get to know your grandchild." I opened my wallet and handed her a picture of Caitlin and Aria.

"Your wife is not Chinese! Are there no Chinese where you live."

"She's Irish Canadian and incredibly beautiful. I am blessed she wanted to marry me. The picture was taken right after Aria was born. She can sit up by herself now."

"I am looking forward to meeting my granddaughter. I have many questions."

"And I have many answers, but we better go to sleep. We leave for Collingwood early in the morning."

"Can you show me Collingwood on a map? You know I like maps."

"I'll show you tomorrow, but now I want you to sleep peacefully, knowing I'll watch over you from now on."

When she squeezed my hand, I relaxed but could hardly believe I was really with my mother. We woke early and walked to the train station, where I purchased our tickets. She held a firm grip on my arm as we walked, and I was overcome by the contented smile on her face as we boarded the train. We had a small room with two seats and two bunks, barely room for the two of us to stand.

On the way to the dining car, I showed her the restroom. She was surprised it had a flush toilet. The trains in China just had a hole opening to the tracks. When we were served breakfast of scrambled eggs and sausage, she tapped the table and looked around, and I asked, "Is there a problem? Would you like something else?"

"Chopsticks."

"In Canada we eat with forks, knives and spoons like Europeans. Let me show you how to hold them." I showed her which hand to use and how to use each utensil. She was awkward and kept dropping food off the fork. "Do you want me to request chopsticks?"

"No. I must adapt to the Canadian way." She watched me eat for a few minutes, then mimicked my movements.

She stopped eating and watched the people in the dining car for several minutes, then asked, "How did you survive in this country?"

"I followed your advice and looked forward because my future was before me. I embraced my new country and learned

English as fast as I could. I'll give you my Chinese/English dictionary so you can learn more English. "

"Your Mandarin is a little slow, but the grammar is good."

"My Mandarin is rusty."

She gazed out the window at the countryside and, after a few minutes, said, "I held the pain of your leaving and was certain I would never see my children again. It took you to bring me across the ocean."

"We're together now, and you can let it go. We'll make up for all the years the locusts have eaten."-

"I lost both my children when they were so young and had to keep my emotions hidden, but I can no longer restrain my tears." She used the napkin to wipe her eyes and said, "Tell me about your journey. Your sponsoring family must have been good to you."

"It was a difficult voyage, and no sponsoring family was waiting for me in Vancouver."

"It tore me up to send you away not knowing who would be receiving you. But, Zhang said..."

"Zhang was part of a human trafficking ring."

"Zhang is scum of the earth. I saw him several times to deliver my letters to you. He told me to stop coming and gave me an address in Vancouver, but I never received a letter from you. I was overwhelmed when your father was imprisoned, and my teaching position was jeopardized. Then the authorities took me away from Lijuan and YeYe," she bowed her head and took a deep breath. "I was sent to the mountains and forbidden to return to Hangzhou. After several years, I gave up hope and tried to make the most of my life teaching children. Then one day, men took me to Hong Kong. Zhang and I boarded a freighter and shared a room. He was abusive and did unspeakable things, prevented me from speaking to anyone or leaving the cabin during the voyage."

"I had no control over who was sent to free you. For years, I tried to find you, Father, YeYe, and Lijuan. My employer hired a private investigator in China several years ago to locate all of you. The investigator said Father was a political prisoner and would never be released, and you had been removed from your job and sent to the mountains, but he never found where."

"What about Lijuan and YeYe?"

"Nothing on YeYe. The same people that found you also located Lijuan. I'm hoping she's on her way here."

"She is alive and coming to Canada? Should we have stayed in Vancouver to wait for her?"

"She's alive, but there was difficulty in getting her out of the country. I must return home to Caitlin and my job but will return to Vancouver if she arrives."

"When will you know?"

"Not until she arrives, just like I received a call two days ago to pick you up."

"I will be anxious until you hear. My sweet Lijuan must have had a difficult life after I was taken away."

"Let's hope that she'll be here soon."

"Tell me about Aria and your wife."

I spent the next few hours telling her about Caitlin and how we met. "Can I see her picture again?" She glowed as she pointed to Aria.

Over the next two days, I told about meeting Kai on the voyage, the prison camp experience with Dung and Tak, our escape to Collingwood, and the adjustment to life as a Chinese man in Canada. She asked about my job, so I told her about

Julian and how he had taken me under his wing. I also told her about Catherine and how she impacted my life.

We were both weary and emotionally exhausted when we pulled into the Collingwood train station Saturday afternoon. Caitlin and Aria were waiting for us on the platform. Caitlin was grinning from ear to ear, and Aria reached her arms out when she saw me. I was overwhelmed and didn't know who to introduce first. I took Aria in my arms, and when I kissed Caitlin on her lips and turned toward Mother, she had her hands over her mouth and said, "You kiss in public?"

I ignored the comment and introduced her to Caitlin and Aria. Mother reached to hold Aria, but my daughter clung to me.

"Mother, she hasn't seen me in five days. Give her time to get familiar with you. She's tired and will probably fall asleep in my arms on the way home."

"I understand. She is prettier than her picture."

"Caitlin, will you drive home so I can hold Aria." I don't want Mother to feel uneasy because Aria won't go to her."

"Tell your mother she can spend the day with her granddaughter tomorrow and meet the rest of our extended family. Look how fast Aria took to Chukee."

"Yes, but Chukee didn't want to hold her; he sang to her. I hope Mother doesn't get her feelings hurt. By the way, Mother said you and Aria are beautiful."

Seeing Caitlin smile warmed my heart.

Not wanting Mother to feel left out of our conversation, I translated most of what Caitlin said. This would be a difficult transition because Mother seemed to have forgotten most of the English she knew, and Caitlin could only say hello, goodbye, and I love you in Mandarin.

When we pulled into the driveway, Mother gasped, and I remembered the first time I saw this magnificent home. We had lived here so long that I forgot about the impression it made on others.

"We're home Mother," I said in Mandarin, then I said home in English and had her say it.

"Is this where you work?" she asked.

"No, Mother. This is where we live. And now, this is where you live."

Aria was sleeping in my arms, so I carried her to bed, and Caitlin took my bag and walked in with Mother.

Rhoda had the table set for dinner and food on the stove, and she was in the parlor with Chukee when I went by on the way to the nursery. By the time I returned to the kitchen, Rhoda had transferred Chukee to his wheelchair, and they were all at the table. I introduced Mother to Rhoda and Chukee, and Mother responded in Mandarin, and Rhoda spoke Filipino to both of them as if they could understand her.

After dinner, Mother insisted on helping with the dishes. Washing dishes was going to be quite different for Mother. Julian had installed a dishwasher, so Caitlin needed to teach her how to use it.

I carried Chukee upstairs and helped Rhoda get him to bed.

"Chukee and your mother are going to be too much for Caitlin," Rhoda said.

"I hope Mother can help with Chukee and Aria so you don't have to work so hard."

"Men are thick, just let me move Chukee to my house. I've grown quite fond of him."

"He likes you!"

She punched me in the arm and said, "It's time for me to go. I'll see you in the morning. Will you take care of Chukee while I go to church with Caitlin?"

"If you take him home, who will watch him while you go out?"

"You can watch him at my house and bring Aria."

"Caitlin likes having you here, and so do I. You're family."

Rhoda and I entered the kitchen as Caitlin and Mother were finishing the dishes.

"Why don't you collect your mother's things and get her settled in her room," Caitlin said.

When I took Mother upstairs to her room, she took hold of my arm and asked, "Where did you get the money to buy this house?"

"This was Julian LeBlanc's home. When he died, he willed it to Caitlin and me. Julian's wife and only son predeceased him, and he adopted me."

"What does adopted mean?"

"It means that officially, on paper, I'm the son of Julian LeBlanc, as far as Canadian law is concerned."

"Are you no longer my son?" She stepped away from me.

"I'm your son and always will be."

"How can you be my son and the son of someone else? And why would you let someone adopt you?"

"It was a difficult decision to make but necessary to become a citizen. Besides this house, I also inherited a bank called Merchant's Bank. It's where I work and how I can afford to keep this house, support Caitlin and Aria, and bring you here."

"I do not understand all these things, but are you still legally my son?"

"In China, yes. There's another layer of complication in Canada, but I'll always be your son, and I'm so glad you're here."

She moved toward me, squeezed my arm, and said, "This is all beyond my understanding, but the last few days have been like a new life for me."

She kissed me on the cheek before I closed her door. I didn't sleep much that night.

Chapter Six

Mother walked into the kitchen before sunrise. I rose and bowed before her, she took my hand, kissed it, then held it against her cheek, and a smile radiated across her face. "I had given up hope of ever seeing you again. Forgive me if I do not want to let go." She slipped her arms around my waist and hugged me like she did when I was small.

"You were always with me, and my heart is bursting with happiness now that you're here," I said.

"I am sorry I doubted you. You are my Tao Wen Shun, but I have not heard anyone call you Wen Shun. Do you have a new name?

"Winson LeBlanc."

"After Julian LeBlanc?"

"Yes."

"LeBlanc is French, but Winston is British like Winston Churchill."

"I wanted an English name that sounded like Wen Shun and changed it on the voyage because I didn't like the name Zhang gave me."

"Ah, I understand. When you come to live in a new country, you are like a new person, so it is fitting you chose a different name, but you should have kept Tao as your surname."

"When Julian adopted me, my surname changed."

"Should I choose a new name?"

"It's your choice. My attorney is preparing papers for you to become a citizen. We should tell him if you choose a new name."

"I have no ideas."

"Lil is your Chinese name and means elegant, pure, and reason. The English word, Lily, is a beautiful white flower. Tao can be your surname, but you don't have to decide today."

"I told you to assimilate, and I need to take my own advice. I like the sound and rhythm of Lily. Yes, I want to be called Lily, Lily Tao."

"Good. Lily Tao, I have tea ready for us."

"I want my son to call me Mother."

"Mother in English or Chinese?"

"In Chinese. I want to hear what you called me when you were young."

"Mother, would you like tea?"

She smiled as she said, "Yes, thank you," in English.

"Very good. The more English words you use, the faster you'll learn." I poured her a cup and asked, "Did you sleep well?"

"No. But it does not matter because I am with my son, who is alive and well, and in the West. It is so different here, not simple like back home. You have so many luxuries like separate bathrooms. In the mountains we sat on a large, water-filled, wooden bucket. Every morning, one of us would empty the contents and scrub the bucket clean with a bamboo brush in a nearby river. It was nice not to have to clean a bucket this morning."

"There's a brush next to the toilet if you want to clean it."

"You have a quick wit. Where are your wife and Aria this morning?"

I noticed she called Aria by name but called Caitlin my wife.

"Caitlin's in the nursery feeding Aria. She'll be in for tea soon."

Mother watched my every move, and when I sat beside her, she said, "You have grown into a handsome young man and look much like a young YeYe."

"I miss him so much. YeYe came to me in a dream when I needed him, in fact, more than once."

"He also comes to me in dreams. There is a collective consciousness about YeYe, you, and me." Her right hand shook and spilled her tea. "I have not seen Lijuan since..." She set her cup in the saucer and couldn't continue.

"Let's hope she'll arrive soon."

After moments of silence, she said, "Show me Collingwood on a map."

I returned from my office with a map and pointed to Collingwood and Vancouver. Then I pointed to Hangzhou to show her the ocean route we had traveled.

"I would have enjoyed seeing the port cities but wasn't allowed out of the cabin. Did you see the cities on your voyage?"

"Unfortunately, I wasn't a passenger, worked below deck, and wasn't allowed off the ship until we arrived in Vancouver."

"Zhang was full of lies."

"Remember, I told you on the train, he was a feeder agent for a Chinese crime ring in British Columbia."

"He is evil and did horrible things to me on the voyage."

My blood began to boil. "What things? Did he ra..." Mother put her hand over my mouth. When she removed it, I said, "I won't ask you about it again, but I'll remember what he did."

"Then I hope you never see him again. Certain things are best forgotten." She looked around the kitchen, at the ceiling height and the crown molding, and said, "This is the largest kitchen I have ever seen. Only a crime ring could afford this house. Are you sure you are not associated with them?"

"I don't work for the Chinese crime ring."

"Then explain this house and all your connections to get me here."

"As I told you, Caitlin and I inherited this house from Julian LeBlanc. He adopted me, and I inherited his estate upon his death. Everything has been legal, but the men who brought us here are criminals, and their business is illegal."

"How did you get me out of China, and why did they bring me to you?"

"Because of Chukee."

We heard Aria babbling as Caitlin carried her into the kitchen, and Mother rose and extended her arms, but when Aria looked at her, she hid her face against Caitlin's shoulder.

"Aria, this is your NaiNai, your Grandmother," Caitlin said as Aria clung to her.

"Your wife knows NaiNai, good," Mother said in Mandarin, then said, "Good morning," in English.

Caitlin turned to me and said, "Your mother knows English?"

"Only a few words." Then I turned to Mother and said, "Caitlin knows a couple of Mandarin phrases."

When Aria reached for me, I took her from Caitlin, and she started playing with my medallion. We sat and talked, and I bounced Aria on my knee while Caitlin prepared breakfast.

"Mother took English classes at university. Hopefully, being around us and hearing us daily, her vocabulary will return."

"I say yes, no, please, thank you, home, understand more," Mother said.

Caitlin said, "Excellent," and Mother repeated, "Excellent."

Caitlin served oatmeal with fruit and walnuts and said, "I hope your mother will enjoy this. Does she want chopsticks?"

"Silverware will do, and she'll be content with anything you fix." When Caitlin sat, Mother said, "Thank you, Caitlin." She pointed to herself and said, "Lily."

"You're welcome, Lily," she said to Mother. Then turned to me and said, "Wow, she picked a new name right away."

"She wants to assimilate."

Aria ate bananas in her highchair and kept pointing at Mother. Caitlin pointed at Mother and said NaiNai, pointed at me and said Daddy, pointed at herself and said Mummy, and pointed at Aria and said Aria. Then Mother repeated the process, and I repeated it after Mother. Aria babbled, and we were waiting for her first words. Mother picked at her oatmeal like she had at every meal so far. She said she regularly ate rice in the mountains, but once a day they had a watery soup.

When she reached her arms to Aria again, Aria responded with outstretched arms. Mother lifted her with a delighted expression and sang to her in Chinese while Aria pulled Mother's hair and giggled excitedly.

"Love, Rhoda said she's going to church with you, so I'll do the dishes while you're at church. If you'll excuse me, I'll tend to Chukee and bring him downstairs."

"I need to get ready. Is it okay for me to leave Aria with your mother?"

"Of course, she'll be overjoyed. I'll tell her." I translated and went upstairs to get Chukee ready for the day. When I returned to the kitchen with Chukee, Mother was still entertaining Aria.

"She reminds me of when Lijuan was a baby. Tell me again what you know about Lijuan?"

"She was taken from home and given to one of Mao's generals, Lin Biao. Men working for the Chinese syndicate will be bring her to Vancouver, but nothing is certain."

"Seeing you leave China was like my bones were pulled from my body. When we returned home from watching you sail away, I had a terrible argument with your father and said mean things to him. As it turned out my actions caused me trouble at school, and I was taken away shortly after your father went to prison."

When Aria patted Mother's face, she smiled and said, "This is my granddaughter."

"I'm glad Aria will grow up knowing her NaiNai Lily. There are toys in her playpen, so take her there while Chukee finishes breakfast, and I clean the kitchen."

"I can help you."

"You can help me by playing with Aria."

She lifted Aria and said, "She needs a clean diaper."

Rhoda walked in the back door, and Aria squealed and reached for her.

"Rhoda, you're just in time. I'm going to show Mother how to change Aria. Can you transfer Chukee to the recliner?"

"And good morning to you. Let me kiss my little girl, and then I'll take care of Chukee. Is Caitlin still going to church?"

"She's getting ready."

While Caitlin and Rhoda were at church, Mother, Chukee, Aria, and I entertained each other in the parlor. Aria enjoyed the attention, but Chukee tired and fell asleep. When he snored, Mother said, "Tell me about Chukee."

"I met him at the work camp. He's the younger brother of the crime boss. He seemed mentally slow and in poor health but liked me from the beginning and called me 'Yiqi' because

I played the xiao. His brother died of cancer about a month ago and, before he died, asked if I would take care of Chukee. In return, he offered to find you and Lijuan and bring you here. He had the right connections, and no one else could have gotten you out of China."

"So you do still work for the syndicate? When will you tell me the truth?"

"I've told you the truth, and it's your choice to believe me or not."

"I want to believe you, but the pieces don't fit together. How did you get me past Mao's army?"

"I don't know and didn't ask. Some things are better left unsaid."

"Chukee doesn't talk much, and his Mandarin is difficult to understand. What's wrong?"

"He has several medical issues and is not expected to live long. He also has a learning disability. Men at the camp called him retarded. All we can do is make his last days comfortable."

"I can help care for him. I am small but sturdy."

"I don't want you to hurt yourself. He's dead weight."

"I worked hard in the fields when I wasn't teaching, often into the night. The night skies in the mountains were beautiful with so many stars, and I imagined you looking at the same sky. Too much time has been stolen from us, but now the stars know we have been reunited."

I loved how she expressed her thoughts and explained her insights. "Tell me about your journey from Hangzhou to the mountains."

"Your father was in prison for about a month when the red guard came into my classroom, shaved my head in front of my students, and arrested me. I was transported in a large truck with about fifty women prisoners, all squashed together like sardines. We were frightened and worried about our families. We drove for hours on winding roads without food and water and were confined to a camp with primitive buildings and grass mats to sleep on. After weeks, a guard took several of us to a nearby school and told us to teach village children how wonderful Mao was and how he was the savior of our country. Of course, we could not speak the truth and only taught Mao's history. But I was fortunate and taught basic science, biology, botany, and astronomy. Everything we said or did was scrutinized, and I thought I would break. If we were caught with tears in our eyes, we were beaten, so we learned to bury our emotions and do our jobs."

"Would our lives have been different had Father not spoken against Mao?"

"Perhaps for a while, but if any of my students told the Red Guards I taught Western ideas, I would have been arrested. So don't blame your father that our lives were irrevocably altered."

"It's hard not to."

"There are reasons things happened. Do you see any way you could have left China on your own? If Zhang had rejected you, Mao's regime would not have allowed you to leave. Instead, you would have been forced to join the army and Communist party or go to prison. The last time I saw your father was the morning he attended his hearing before the council. Mao broke everyone to his will."

"What I experienced on the ship and in Canada almost broke me. But we wouldn't be together today if I hadn't taken the voyage."

"You had a purpose written in the stars. When I told you not to look back, I wanted you to succeed in your new country, to move forward. I taught girls in my classroom to set goals and keep their eyes on the future. That's why so many went to university. You did not settle for a life that was less than you were capable of living. Do you remember the wise man who blessed you on the way to the ship?"

"Each time I went with YeYe to the docks to pick up a shipment of snake skins, we stopped and gave alms to him. He blessed me because of YeYe."

"The chances you took, the people you met, and those you loved have shaped your life. It was in your heart to help others from when you were young."

"It's time for our hearts to heal."

"Being without you was hard for YeYe and me."

"What about Lijuan?"

"She grieved for you and clung to your father. She was inconsolable when he was taken away."

"I hope we receive news of her arrival soon."

"Soon is a strange word. What does it mean?" She put her hands over her mouth and then clasped them together. "This is too much at one time for an old woman."

"You look as lovely now as the day I departed."

"You realize that was eighteen years ago?"

"Yet it feels like yesterday."

"I need to do something to busy myself."

"Let's make congee."

"Do you eat rice porridge in Canada?"

"Not at restaurants. I made it for Julian when he refused to eat, and he liked it. I also make it for Aria. It was her first solid food, but I made it runny and without much spice."

Chukee snored so loud in the recliner we laughed as we passed him to put Aria down for her morning nap. When we returned to the kitchen, Mother chopped garlic, ginger, and coriander while I cleaned up and started the rice.

"I feel comfortable for the first time in years, and it is as if YeYe is here. You are so much like him. He loved you as the son he always wanted."

"He was everything to me." I wanted to say, like a father but didn't want to show any disrespect.

We were cleaning up when I heard a car pull into the driveway, and a few minutes later, Caitlin and Rhoda came in the back door.

"Smells like you're making congee. Aria will be happy," Caitlin said.

"We just finished. How was church?"

"It was a wonderful sermon about Joseph being restored with his father. We talked about it the other day: what Satan meant for evil, God meant for good."

"I'd like to hear the whole story later."

"If you'll excuse me, it's time for Chukee's meds," Rhoda said.

"He's been sleeping in the parlor for about an hour."

Rhoda left to tend to Chukee.

"Mother and Kathleen are bringing lunch. They knew we'd be busy with Lily, so they put a turkey in the oven. They'll be here in about an hour. Would you set the table while I change my clothes? There'll be enough food to invite Kai and Wei Lei, and Lily might enjoy meeting them."

I put my arms around her. "Love, you're the most thoughtful person I know."

"When Caitlin left the kitchen, Mother said, "Are you always so affectionate with your wife? You did not learn that from your father and me."

"Caitlin is my world, and I like to let her know how much I love and appreciate her. I'm sorry if it bothers you, but I don't intend to stop. Canadians are more demonstrative with their feelings."

We had a full house for lunch, and I introduced Lily to everyone. Conversations took place in Chinese and English, and there were smiles and laughter. Caitlin asked Wei Lei if she would go shopping with Lily and her to buy new clothes and shoes. When Wei Lei told Mother, Mother said, "I don't need clothes, but I have not had new shoes since I left Hangzhou." I asked Wei Lei to find her comfortable slippers to wear around the house and good walking shoes.

After supper, Mother and I took Aria for a walk while the ladies cleaned the dishes, and Kai offered to help Rhoda give Chukee a shower. We had to bathe him downstairs because the shower was a walk-in and built for a disabled person.

During our walk, Mother asked, "Caitlin's mother was at dinner with us, but not her father. Is he still angry?"

"Her father passed away not too long ago. He was a difficult man, but he loved Caitlin, and Aria was the apple of his eye. He loved spending time with her, and I'm sorry she'll not remember him, but I'm delighted she'll know you."

"Me too. I am happy you have such a pleasing family and friends."

We walked to the harbor and sat on a bench, so Aria could watch the geese and ducks. After long moments of silence, Mother asked, "Did you ever give up on finding us?"

"It was always in my mind, but for years, all my energy went into surviving. It was Julian who created the opportunity to even search for you."

"Tell me more about him."

"He was an amazing man, kind and generous, and I cherished every day with him. He told me that I must build bridges, not walls between people. He believed the world is all about building long-term relationships, and his father taught him that nothing is more important than a man's honor and a good name. Reputation was your most valuable asset, and your name reflected your character. YeYe taught me the same principles."

"They would have liked each other."

"I told Julian about YeYe, you, Father, and Lijuan. He hired a Chinese private investigator named Howard Wong, to search for you. I'll let you read Mr. Wong's letters reporting on his searches and conditions in China. He sent another investigator to our Hangzhou home, who found another family living there, and they had pages from your journal, which he sent to me."

Arriving home, I took her into my office and gave her the pages from her journal. She clutched them to her chest and asked if she could keep them.

When Aria was asleep for her afternoon nap, we sat in the parlor sharing stories. I was happy to see Kai and Wei Lei engage with Mother. Kai asked many questions about China, but Mother didn't have many answers. Instead, she preferred to talk about their lives in Canada.

When we went to bed, Caitlin and I were exhausted. We hadn't had much time to talk to each other but were so tired that when the alarm went off in the morning, I was still curled around her in the same position we had fallen asleep.

"How are you doing with Lily?" I asked.

"We'll be fine. She's like me and needs to stay busy. She enjoys helping with Aria, and I'll show her how to give Aria a bath this morning. We'll pick up Wei Lei and leave Aria with

Catherine and Yves at ten o'clock. Catherine always asks for more time with Aria. She might miss her morning nap but may sleep longer in the afternoon. Do you mind if I introduce Lily to Catherine and Yves without you?"

"I could meet you there at ten o'clock."

"That'd be nice." She put her arms around me and kissed my lips, bringing a smile to both our faces.

Chapter Seven

After getting Chukee up and visiting with Mother for a while, I went to the bank, and Peggy was sitting at my desk and asked about my mother.

"She's adjusting but didn't want me to leave this morning. I'm going to meet her and Caitlin at ten o'clock."

"If I hadn't seen my son in eighteen years, I'd want to spend a great deal of time with him too."

"Any pressing business I should know about?"

"Two men came in to see you last week, one on Thursday and the other on Friday. The first was a short Chinese man, who was smartly dressed in an expensive-looking suit, but I was surprised to see his black hair slicked back in a ponytail. He said he was new to the area, starting a business, and was turned away by First Simco Bank."

"I'm not surprised. Did he give his name or leave a card?"

"No. I offered to make an appointment, and he said he was on his way out of town and would contact you on his return trip. The second man said his name was Mezzetti."

"Mick Mezzetti?"

"I don't know. He went to Janet's window, and she didn't recognize the name. Anita or I would've asked. Janet said he wanted to meet you in person. She made a face and said he was dark-skinned, tall, with yellowed, crooked teeth."

I was stunned to hear Mick Mezzetti was out of jail and dared to walk into my bank since Mezzetti and Patrick Chorley had planned Caitlin and Kathleen's kidnapping. Chorley confessed and was sentenced to fifteen years while Mezzetti was still awaiting trial. I called Chief Kirkpatrick, and as far as he knew, bail had not been granted because Mezzetti was a flight risk. But, like Tak, maybe he had an attorney with connections to a judge who allowed bail. Mick should've been in jail.

I arrived at Catherine's before Caitlin, Aria, and Mother. When they entered the kitchen, Aria squealed as she pointed toward Catherine, who held her arms out and said, "Let me hold my darling girl." She took her and kissed her on one cheek, and Yves kissed her on both cheeks.

I introduced Lily to them and translated for Mother, who looked somewhat uncomfortable. To my surprise, Yves said in Mandarin, "It's a pleasure to meet you, Lily."

Mother's eyes widened, and I asked Yves, "How do you know Mandarin?"

"I toured with a Chinese violinist. He taught me Mandarin, and I taught him French."

Mother responded to him in French, "A pleasure to meet you." He looked as amazed as I did. Caitlin tugged on my arm and whispered, "She speaks fluent French to Yves but can't speak English?"

"I'm as surprised as you. I'll ask Mother later."

We had an international group in the kitchen with three languages spoken. When Wei Lei joined us, I excused myself and returned to the bank.

Anita came into my office late in the afternoon and said, "There's a man in the lobby asking to speak with you."

"Did you get his name?"

"No, but I think it's Mezzetti. He was here Friday and spoke to Janet."

"Will you ask Gene to come into my office?"

"Sir, I'm sorry, but I told Gene it was okay to leave early. He went to the bus station to pick up his wife."

"It's not a good idea to leave the bank without security. Clear it with Peggy or me before you do it again. Send the man in."

I was short with Anita and uneasy as she led a tall, burly man wearing a shiny grey suit and alligator boots into my office. He had dark eyes and a scowl on his pock-marked face. I stood to meet him and had to look up. "Sir, I'm Winson LeBlanc. What can I do for you?"

"My name's Frankie, Frankie Mezzetti." He was fidgeting, and his shirt was unbuttoned to the middle of his chest, revealing a two-inch gold cross on a thick gold chain. "I have a brother named Mick."

I didn't want to be alone with this man. Thankfully Peggy appeared at the door with her purse over her arm.

"Please have a seat and excuse me for a minute, Mr. Mezzetti. I need to speak to one of my employees before she leaves for the day. Peggy, a word, please."

I kept my eye on him as I walked into the hall and quietly asked Peggy to call the Ontario Provincial Police (OPP) to send an officer, no sirens, as we might have a problem.

"Mr. Mezzetti, please have a seat."

"You ain't from here, eh." His mouth pulled to the right as he spoke.

"I'm from China." I watched him cautiously as I sat in my chair. "What can I do for you?"

"You put my brother Mick in the pen; you surely did. And I apologize for what he done to your wife and her friend. But you see, me and my brother don't get along. He went one way, and I went another. We're oil and water and don't mix. You got me."

"It's kind of you to apologize, but not necessary." I hoped my sigh wasn't audible.

"You can relax. I've another reason to see you. My best friend, Mario Comenga, and me want to open an Italian restaurant. Max Gilpin said to see Mr. LeBlanc at Merchants Bank; that's you."

"Tell me more about your plans."

"I own a house on Fourth Street, one block off Hurontario. Mario's a great chef and has operated Italian restaurants in Toronto and Sault Saint Marie. He and his wife, Teresa, recently moved here. We're calling the restaurant Brunello's."

"If Max sent you, that's a good sign. Our business provides capital and expertise to help start and grow businesses." I opened a drawer and handed him two applications. "We need you and Mr. Comenga to fill out these loan applications. Peggy Baker is the Vice President of commercial lending and will work with you both. Here's Peggy's card, and I'll tell her to expect you."

"Gilpin said you was a good man."

I walked him out as two OPP officers walked in. Frankie turned to me and asked, "Was you expecting trouble from me?"

"Nothing personal, just trying to keep everyone safe."

He laughed as he waved his hand and said, "Arrivederci!"

∽

On the way home from work, I stopped for flowers. The daylight was getting longer, but it was dark when I walked through the backdoor. Mother was in the kitchen having tea, and her face lit up when I handed her the flowers. "For me? Oh my! They are beautiful! Thank you, my son. It feels good to say the words 'my son' and see your face at the same time."

"And for me to stand before you and say the word, Mother. I'm so glad you're here."

I embraced her and was lost in the moment until I noticed how silent the house was.

"Where are Caitlin and Rhoda?"

"Caitlin is in the nursery with Aria. I helped Rhoda take Chukee upstairs. He did not have a good afternoon, so he will not be at dinner."

"Thank you for giving Caitlin privacy to breastfeed Aria and helping Rhoda with Chukee."

We sat at the table, and she lifted her feet and smiled as she wiggled them before me. "I have new slippers. I've never had anything like this on my feet. I may never take them off."

"If you want to go outside, I hope you bought something more practical, too."

"Caitlin and Wei Lei helped me pick out warm boots and casual shoes. Caitlin spent too much money on me today."

"Did you buy dresses?"

"She kept asking me to try several of them on, but I told her what Mr. Yonge bought me was sufficient. All your wife wanted was to buy me garments; she spends too much money."

"I asked her to take good care of you."

"Then you spend too much money. There are so many who are starving back home. I had one Mao suit and one pair of boots for eighteen years. I saw women trying on many dresses, and buying three or four."

"You're in a different country now. There's no way to send money to China, and if we did, it would go to Mao or his agents."

"Many people asked about Aria and made comments to Caitlin. I wish I knew what they said."

"Maybe that gives you more incentive to learn English. You spoke fluent French to Yves; when did you learn French?"

"I speak about the same amount of French as English. I learned from books and had a professor who taught us French when we read Albert Camus' famous essay *The Myth of Sisyphus*."

"Catherine had me read his book *The Plague*. What was his essay about?"

"Coping with life in a universe without meaning. He compared our situation to that of Sisyphus, an ancient Greek myth character condemned for eternity to push a boulder up a mountain, only to roll back down when it reaches the top. The professor felt that was what it was like to want to learn in China compared to Europe. When your father found out about him, he became angry. Will you tell me about *The Plague*?"

"Now you have the freedom to learn. I'll give you my copy to read, and we can talk about it like I did with Catherine."

"Learning is slower for me after being in the mountains. A few English words are returning, but I am not ready to make sentences. How could Catherine teach you to read when she is blind?

"I read to her, although she can read in braille. Reading out loud helped me learn English faster."

"Wei Lei was upset at one saleslady because she did not want to wait on us."

"There's still prejudice in Canada. Many people walk by me as if I am invisible. I hope it'll change in time."

"Wei Lei stayed for a while this afternoon asking questions about China."

"I have questions too, when you're ready to talk."

"What do you want to know?"

"What happened in Hangzhou after I left?"

Her lower lip trembled as she stared out the window for what seemed like minutes. "Our lives were difficult. You witnessed how it was unsafe on the streets, but events escalated, people were gripped with constant fear of Mao's officials, and life became more difficult each day. One day the red guard came to Lijuan's school and questioned several students in her class. She was so frightened we let her stay home with YeYe. The next day I was arrested and never saw them again."

"A few years ago, I had a strange vision. Sitting on the bench by the blue spruce in the backyard, I was in total distress over Caitlin and her father. This was before we were married. YeYe came to me and said he was no longer walking on earth but would always be with me. He reminded me to be who I was created to be. When he walked away, he was with NaiNai, and they waved at me. It may have been an out-of-body experience or something from my subconscious, but it doesn't matter because it was real to me."

"YeYe told me his spirit went with you the day you left, and I can see he is still alive in you."

"Did you have friends in the mountains?"

"We worked in the rice fields, and were discouraged from talking with each other, so we whispered at night. I never expected to return to civilization. We lived in squalor and disease, but I enjoyed my students and became quite fond of a few of them."

"How did Zhang get you away from the guards."

"Three men came into my classroom and took me by force. They put me in a large trunk in the back of a truck and took me to Zhang. He was in Hong Kong, and we boarded a freighter with false papers. He didn't tell me where we were going or why. I will not speak about the journey."

She looked relieved when Caitlin came into the kitchen with Aria. Mother stretched out her arms, and Aria went to her willingly.

Mother tried to say a few English words to Caitlin and Rhoda during dinner, and when Mother and I were doing the dishes, she wanted to know more about Catherine. When I told her how she became my surrogate for her, she said, "I hoped you would find favor and be led to those who would guide you. Catherine's music and council were what I desired for you. And Julian, for him to build this home and take you as his son, I wish I could have met him."

"He was special, living through his physical condition and carrying the weight of all his responsibilities. Like YeYe and you, he taught me so much about life and character. It's as if I've lived many lives: one in China, another in captivity, one being mentored by Catherine, one as Julian's son, another married to Caitlin and fatherhood, and now being reunited with you."

Her eyes were about to shut, and she said, "I am tired and need to retire, and you need to spend time alone with Caitlin and Aria." She kissed me on both cheeks and said, "Good night, Canadian style."

In our bedroom, Caitlin asked, "What did your mother say about shopping today?"

"She appreciated your taking her and wanting to buy clothes for her."

"All she wanted was shoes!"

"She does love those slippers. When you haven't had anything new in eighteen years, it's hard to adjust. The two dresses David bought her are enough for now. Next, we must work on her hygiene and washing her clothes. She's been living in primitive conditions, and in her eyes, we're wasteful. Give her time to adjust."

Chapter Eight

Caitlin had a doctor's appointment for Aria, so I went home for lunch and stayed with Mother until Wei Lei came to spend the afternoon with her.

When I returned to the bank, Peggy said, "Darvin Avant was here and asked to speak privately with me in my office after he opened an account with $100 cash."

"I'm sure he had an ulterior motive. Did he try to hire you again?"

"He was surprised to see I had my own office, pointed to the Vice President below my name on the door, and asked how much of a raise I received with my promotion. I said it was none of his business. I wasn't inclined to tell him anything after he schemed to take the bank from you by leaking information to the paper. He said I'd have more opportunities working for a Canadian-owned bank. Before leaving, he criticized the way I wore my hair."

"Probably to aggravate you like he does me. You look professional and well-groomed to me."

"Thank you. I don't like him, he's creepy, and when I told him I hoped to spend my entire career at Merchants, he grunted and said in his high nasal tone that it would be a short career."

"I appreciate you telling me about your conversation."

"I watched him walk through the bank like he owned it. He's so arrogant. How can he be like that? I would never work for him."

"He does what he does because he can. His father was worse from what I hear. You're an accomplished banking professional with excellent management skills, and I hope we have a long future together."

"You've been generous with my salary increases and promotions. But not just me. You've provided advancement opportunities to women who work here and treat us with respect, which we never received under Mr. Taylor."

"Julian taught me about meritocracy, and I'll endeavor to provide an environment that rewards those who desire to grow to their potential and receive equal pay regardless of their sex or ethnicity."

"I see the payroll records, and you raise staff salaries before your own."

"Julian also taught me to put the customers and staff first. Diamonds don't shine at the bottom of a cave. They require a change agent like a jeweler who knows how to cut and polish to change a rough diamond into a shaped and faceted gemstone. You have responded well to instruction and learned from the hard knocks you've taken. If you get values right, everything else falls into place."

Peggy had a scholarly disposition, possessed impeccable character, and could perform any function in the bank. I knew she had leadership potential and wanted to develop her like Julian did with me.

Over the next few days, we had a series of accounts opened with the minimum deposit, and the common thread in their personal histories was their occupation at Avant's First Simco Bank. I scheduled a meeting with Clive Owen for Friday afternoon.

We exchanged pleasantries, and Clive asked about Lily.

"She's adjusting. She loves Aria and is trying her best to speak English. She and Caitlin still have difficulty communicating, but they're both trying. Every day Mother asks about Lijuan, but Eng said they're having difficulty getting her out of China."

"Hopefully, you'll hear good news soon." He cleared his throat and said, "I have unpleasant news I need to share with you. I received two letters from Darvin Avant. First, as the Registrar of Merchant's Bank advising me he's purchased stock from Oliver Taylor and to reregister and reissue the shares to Darvin Avant. The stock certificate was included and endorsed by Taylor."

"I didn't know Taylor owned stock in the bank."

He handed me a document titled, 'Capitalization Table' and said, "It's a small ownership percentage. It was a short list of the stockholders. First, it had Julian's name, then Taylor and Clive owned two and one-half percent each.

"When the bank was chartered, Julian offered me stock in the bank in return for my serving as General Council. Taylor was hired as president, and after working for the bank for a year, he threatened to quit unless he was granted stock. I take the blame for failing to include a provision in the corporate charter that Merchants Bank would have the right of first refusal if Taylor wanted to sell his shares. There's no excuse for my error. When the embezzlement occurred, I made another mistake and didn't address the issue of Taylor's stock. I'll reimburse you whatever it costs to purchase Avant's stock." Clive rubbed his forehead thoughtfully with his palm as if it were an eraser trying to change what he should've done.

"Clive, there's no blame, understood? You've done more for me than I could ever repay. We'll work out this problem together and talk about the cost later. Can we buy back the shares at book value or at a premium over book value?"

"There's no provision in the charter to force a shareholder to sell. I'm looking into the law regarding equitable remedies for egregious behavior, unjust enrichment, crimes of dishonesty, rescission, and grounds to rescind ownership. We filed a civil suit against Taylor for embezzlement, and it remains open. We could seek to obtain a default judgment against Taylor because he hasn't appeared in court nor denied our claims. We can also assert Taylor's stock conveyance to Avant was an additional attempt to defraud the bank. We may need to prove Avant had notice of Taylor's intent and would need a witness or a form of communication between Taylor and Avant. He has more up his sleeve. The second letter requests notice of the next shareholder meeting and an agenda item to review executive compensation."

"Is it his right when the shares haven't been transferred?"

"This is a nuisance tactic on Avant's part. You can outvote him on any issue. So let's not get ahead of ourselves."

"He'd be hard-pressed to file a complaint about my salary. I've never given myself a raise."

"A shareholder has the right to examine the books and question your compensation. Based on industry standards, you're not overpaid. He probably pays himself twice your salary."

"Do we know when Avant purchased the shares?"

"In the last thirty days. I'll put Matthew on it to follow the money and determine if we can file a complaint against Avant with the Office of the Inspector General of Banks."

Then I told Clive about Avant opening an account, followed by several of his employees doing the same, and about his attempt to hire Peggy and her response.

"Avant is cunning and methodical. He's frustrated with how the newspaper turned on him and how you stood up to him. He must also be concerned with his loss of customers and market share. As prejudiced as he is, having you own a bank in his marketplace must gall him. He's arrogant, like his father, and walks through the world like he owns it. It might help you to know that his father, Morris, got his start selling lots and carrying notes to finance the sale. He made so many high-interest-rate loans for hard-to-finance properties that he opened a small bank, which was shunned by anyone with a decent net worth. Lewis Thacker's First Simco was the largest bank in town, and Thacker was a quiet man with a passion for sailing. He was last seen crossing a narrow section of the bay aboard his sloop, and a week later, his bloated and decomposing body was found floating offshore near Meaford with a gunshot wound in the back of his head. The boat was never found. Within months, Morris took over First Simco. Like his father, Darvin is a bully narcissist, and since his father's death, I've heard his employees and even his family are intimidated by him."

"My grandfather told me to deal with a bully, you must confront him. Since Taylor is wanted for embezzlement, and Avant has contacted him to purchase these shares, shouldn't he turn Taylor's location over to the RCMP?"

"You'd make a good attorney. It's a sound idea and one I'll address with the OPP and the RCMP. Looking back, I should've recommended a motion to offset the amount Taylor embezzled against the value of his stock." Clive rubbed his fingers across the bridge of his nose as he grimaced.

"This will not impede us. As you said, his ownership strategy is a nuisance, but it has revealed Avant's intent and a possible way to locate Taylor."

"We can legally challenge the conveyance of stock to Avant and threaten an investigation of his aiding and abetting a wanted felon. It's time for me to visit with Chief Kirkpatrick and the RCMP regarding Mr. Avant."

The following morning, Avant came into the bank, and when Anita led him into my office, there were no pleasantries. He walked around looking at the photos on the wall, then sat in front of my desk. One minute, two, another went by, and neither of us said a word.

"I own stock in your bank and want to buy your shares."

"Why don't you sell me your Simco stock?"

"Disgusting!"

I met his stare.

His upper lip curled, then twitched, as he said, "There's talk of a policy change in banking regulations to only allow naturally born Canadians to own banks, so it's only a matter of time before you'll be forced to divest ownership of Merchants."

"By naturally born, don't you mean only white Canadians?"

"You can't change your skin color." His wry smile irritated the hell out of me. "I'll pay a premium for it, but if you wait until you're forced to sell, I'll get it for a song. So I'm doing you a favor by telling you now of impending legislation."

"I don't believe there's any such legislation being considered. Even if there was, and it should pass, you'd be bidding against other banks, and prices at an open auction would be higher than what you offer me today."

"You're impossible." He raised his voice and slammed his hand on my desk, his heavy gold ring cracking against the wood surface like a thunderclap. He rose and shook his fist at me. "Damn it, sell to me!"

"My shares aren't for sale."

"Why?"

"I like owning the bank. Julian believed in me and my ability to run this bank. I would never disappoint him and sell my stock."

"LeBlanc is dead. He has no family, so what does it matter?"

"It matters to me."

The red in his face darkened. "I spent my youth, my adult life, my waking hours to honor an oath to my father, and I'll be damned if I let you stand in our way," he cleared his throat, and the veins in his neck protruded as he leaned toward me, "or block my path to fulfill my destiny."

I rose, walked around the desk, and stood toe to toe with him. "When your father died, he took nothing with him to the grave. Like chess pieces that all go back in the box at the end of a game."

"What the hell, are you spouting off a far east proverb?"

"It's Italian."

"Whatever. The old man should've sold me Merchant's Bank when I made a generous offer in his hospital room."

"Damn, you! You went to his hospital bed to take advantage of a helpless man in critical condition. You're despicable!"

"He was an invalid and couldn't run the bank, his son was worthless, and Cheek was incompetent. It was a matter of time before Merchants would have closed. But then, he found Taylor, and you know how that worked out. My family has been in banking in Collingwood for three generations, so we know how to control banking in Canada!"

I was fuming inside but held my emotions in check. "Julian and his father started with nothing and grew their business by serving the community. Customers you wouldn't serve came to Merchants, grew their companies, and now their children do business with us. Even after his accident, Julian stayed involved in the business. He was committed to using the time he had left to positively impact Collingwood."

"That's all bullshit. The point is you don't have what it takes to succeed in banking. So mark my words, you'll fail, and I'll eventually end up with this bank."

"That's your opinion. I intend to succeed."

"I know all about you and the Chinese syndicate you're part of. I've had someone watching you for years."

He was more devious than I realized, but then I started to put together something that bothered me for a long time. "Did Jay Metzger work for both you and Taylor?"

"What do you think?"

"Metzger should be jailed for sexual assault. You both probably have the same fraternal connections." Metzger followed me for years. He was a predator and was never arrested for his sexual assault on Wei Lei, even after she reported it to the OPP.

"I've also hired Sargent Ellarby as one of my guards."

Ellarby was the OPP officer who investigated me on a frivolous rape charge when I was dating Caitlin. He pursued me without grounds and refused to search for the thugs who had beat me to unconsciousness. If Metzger, Taylor, Ellarby, and Avant were all part of the same fraternal organization composed of policemen, attorneys, and politicians, which

Joseph Lawrence spoke about, none of them had ever been charged with a crime. Ellarby had access to police investigations, which would explain the newspaper leaks from the OPP about Merchant's Bank when Caitlin was kidnapped.

With force, I poked my finger into his chest and said, "You're nothing but a scoundrel, a viper, and someday all your evil ways will be exposed."

He pushed my arm away, cupped his fist in front of my face, and said, "You don't know who you're up against. I never lose! Your owning this bank has upset the natural order, but the order always survives." His voice rose with every word.

"It's time for you to leave."

His soulless eyes searched me like he was looking through my skin, and his eyes scanned my desk like he belonged behind it. He abruptly turned, walked toward the door, stopped, then turned back to face me and said, "The worst form of inequality is to try to make unequal things equal."

"Don't ever come into my office again!"

He took a couple of steps toward me, stopped, pointed his finger at me, and said, "You should consider the welfare of your wife and baby and try to make their lives easier than they are now or will be. Don't endanger them because of your pride and stubbornness."

I stepped toward him and said, "Are you threatening my family and me?" A sort of unsettled, raw energy surged within me.

"You'll find out in due time. I can make your life a living hell."

"Get out of my bank! I'm closing your account and those of your employees. No one threatens my family or me, and I'm calling Chief Kirkpatrick," I shouted.

"Call anyone you want. I'm going to own this bank with or without your consent!" He stormed out of my office.

A minute later, Peggy came into my office and said, "I heard the shouting, then Avant came into the reception area, paced back and forth, muttering to himself and flailing his arms. What did you say to him to create such a ruckus?"

"I told him I wouldn't sell the bank to him, and we're closing his account and those of his employees. Mail checks to them today."

"I say, good riddance!"

After she left, I closed the door, poured a shot of Macallan, and then had a second.

Chapter Nine

It was routine for Mother to be waiting when I came home from work, and one evening I was surprised when I heard in English, "Welcome home, Winson."

"Perfect, Mother. This is the first time you've called me Winson."

"Thank you, Winson."

"You're welcome, Lily." I smiled, and so did she, but that was the extent of her English as she continued in Mandarin.

"I am becoming accustomed to saying Winson, but adjusting to the food is more difficult."

"I realize you're making many adjustments to your new surroundings. For years I craved one more meal with you, to see you cooking, to experience the smells of your recipes and the color of the food, to eat with chopsticks and hear the table talk, help YeYe around the workshop, and smell the wood and sawdust. But I set those thoughts aside because you told me to embrace my new country."

"Because your future was in front of you. I made you promise, and you kept it."

Her eyes turned glossy, and I gave her my handkerchief, then took her by the hand into my office and gave her a flat box with a yellow ribbon tied around it.

"This is another promise I made to you."

Her thin fingers felt the texture of the box, then she slowly opened the top and looked at me with a startled expression. "Silk stockings!"

"I bought them long ago but didn't know where to send them. Go upstairs and put them on."

"I would like to, but there is no way of holding them up," she giggled.

"I'm pretty naïve when it comes to women's clothing. Caitlin can buy whatever you need."

While Caitlin was getting Aria ready for bed, Mother and I sat on the wooden porch swing. She held my hand, and put her head on my shoulder.

"You taught me much about the night sky. I love looking at the moon and the stars. This is a good time of year to see the Milky Way, maybe even the northern lights."

"Have you seen the Aurora Borealis? I taught about these lights in school and hoped to see them one day."

"The first time I saw them was on the ship the night before we entered Vancouver harbor, and I've seen them here many times over the years."

She hummed and rocked, then asked, "Did you write in the journal I gave you?"

"Every day on the ship but not much in the logging camp because of the guards. I still journal, but life has presented so many challenging situations that demanded all my energy to survive that writing hasn't been a priority, and I've realized that it's a luxury."

"Will you let me read them?"

I hesitated before I answered. "I'll give you the journals written in Mandarin tomorrow, but it may be emotional for you because I wrote about difficult times."

"I don't want to pry, but I want to understand what you endured."

"We both had challenging times on each side of the ocean."

We swung quietly for a few minutes until Mother said, "The stars look as if they are hanging a few feet above the ground. It is so peaceful here. Is this heaven?"

"No, it's Collingwood. But wherever you are feels like heaven when you're loved. Catherine said love and hope are the one constant throughout the years and ages, and those moments mark time."

Chapter Ten

On the first of May, Kai picked up Mother to have a Chinese dinner Wei Lei prepared, and Rhoda fed Chukee and put him to bed. Caitlin and I were eating together while Aria played in the corner of the kitchen. She was learning to crawl and loved opening the cabinets. Caitlin rearranged the lower cabinets for Aria's safety and made one up for her to pull everything out. She loved climbing into the empty cupboard and would squeal with delight.

"I took Lily and Aria to see Catherine today. It was a lovely day for a walk, and we had tea and a pleasant time despite the language barrier. Both Aria and Lily were thrilled when Catherine played *Flight of the Bumblebees.* Aria crawled to the piano and was mesmerized by watching Catherine's fingers fly over the keys. When I stepped toward the piano to keep Aria from getting in the way, Catherine stopped playing and asked me to put Aria on her lap. Aria put her tiny fingers on the keys, and we all laughed as she mimicked Catherine's fingering."

"We've added a little musician to our family."

"Catherine had a coughing spell, so Lily made her hot tea with lemon and honey, which helped."

"I'll visit her tomorrow. I owe so much to Catherine. She helped me understand the world and encouraged me to learn."

"We both owe her a great deal. She wanted to quit teaching when she married Yves and have me take over her students, but Aria was born, and I haven't wanted to teach. Maybe I should reconsider."

The next day during lunch, I went to see Catherine. As soon as I walked into the room and before I said a word, she said, "Ah, Winson, welcome, my son."

"I'm wearing a different cologne to mask my scent, and I tiptoed in, yet you still knew it was me. Do you have eyes in the back of your head?"

"I do, but those eyes are blind as well as those in front! Your cologne betrayed you. It was nice to see Lily yesterday."

"She enjoyed the time with you, especially your piano playing. Mother loves music, and I heard Aria loved it too."

"Aria has a natural inclination toward the piano. We tapped the keys and sang songs. I taught Lily *Itsy Bitsy Spider*, so she can sing to Aria in English."

"Will you teach it to me?"

We spent the next fifteen minutes practicing until I memorized the song. It was like old times.

When I asked about Yves, she said, "He's playing cello with a string quartet this afternoon and is playing at a candlelight concert this weekend. They're playing a mix of Vivaldi's *Four Seasons* and several of Astor Piazzolla's compositions. Would you like to go?"

"Of course. I can bring Lily and Caitlin, and we'll pick you up."

"That'd please Yves and me. And bring Aria to visit us more often; she's growing so fast. But I warn you, Grandparents are allowed to spoil their grandchildren, so she may become a little terror when we send her home." Her belly wiggled when she laughed.

"I hope you'll teach her to play piano one day."

"Caitlin can teach her. I don't have the energy I used to have."

"A parent isn't always the best teacher, and I know how much you love teaching."

"I'll make an exception for Aria."

"Caitlin is considering teaching again."

"She should. She has a special rapport with students and is a talented pianist. Besides, I need her to take over with my students."

"Is Joseph home? I haven't seen him for weeks."

"His former fiancée, Julia, returned to town and is staying with an aunt. She called him and came to the house one afternoon. She and Joseph sat for hours talking about what had happened in their lives since they broke up. Joseph told me something rekindled between them, and it was as if they hadn't missed a beat since their parting. Now, he spends every day with her."

"Another reawakened romance?"

"Timing! Joseph and Yves are the only men I know who get younger as they age." Catherine laughed. "You do know old age comes at a bad time," she added as she reached for my hand and said, "You changed my thinking. Watching how you changed, overcame stigmas, and adapted helped me finally deal with my suppressed feelings for Yves."

"I'm happy I could contribute something positive to your life."

"In more ways than I've mentioned."

Joseph Lawrence walked in as I was leaving. He had shaved his beard and traded his thick horn-rimmed glasses for a new stylish design.

"Catherine said someone special came to Collingwood looking for you. I almost didn't recognize you."

"Catherine can't keep a secret. It was an unexpected visit from a girlfriend I hadn't seen in a long time." His face brightened as he said, "I wanted to marry her, but there were complications, and we were heartbroken. I lost myself in Scotch and consumed myself with work, but the void remained."

"What happened to her after your breakup?"

"Her father sent her to live with his sister in Toronto. She wrote several times, but I never replied. She eventually married, but her husband died a few years ago, and I'm delighted she's back in my life."

Chapter Eleven

Maureen had spent several weeks visiting her sister, Evelyn, in Windsor, Ontario, and when she returned to Collingwood, Caitlin invited her for dinner. Maureen came early and entertained Aria with Mother, and although Mother didn't understand most of what Maureen said, they tried to communicate. Maureen went home after dinner, and Mother and I sat on the porch swing, enjoying the cool evening air while Caitlin put Aria to bed.

"Who do you think Aria looks like? She has my eye color." Mother said.

"Does it matter who she looks like? I want her to be happy. It's hard being Chinese in this country."

"She has your blood. Be proud of your heritage."

"I'm proud, but I had issues with Caitlin's father over how Aria would look. I'm glad she's healthy."

"I wish your father could meet her."

"I had a difficult time understanding him."

"Your Father lost his parents at a young age and was tormented by war memories from seeing many of his friends die. A brutal war changes people in ways we cannot comprehend. After he returned from the war, he was a shadow of the man I knew before. He would curl up in bed from nightmares and had constant headaches. I suggested he see a doctor, but he adamantly refused. I loved your father and wanted to help him, and my parents were supportive and kind to let us live with them."

"Tell me how you met Father."

"We were students at university and seemed to have much in common, but he left school to fight the Japanese, and we promised to marry after he returned from war. Our marriage was dry, and our interests and attitudes grew in different directions. He was possessive of me after you were born, and his discipline of you bordered on cruelty, so I made an agreement with him. I would be responsible for disciplining and raising you, and in return, I cooperated with his needs."

This was the first time she shared her personal issues with me. My earliest memories were of Father becoming enraged over something I did, striking me with a belt until my skin welted, and Mother standing between us to shield me from his rage and talking to him until he withdrew. Father could be explosive. I began to understand the stress Mother was up against.

"I'm sorry for the way he treated you. I asked him to appreciate the incredible son we had, but he couldn't do it."

"We lived in the same house but barely knew each other. He didn't involve himself in my life or provide encouragement or guidance. I've wondered what caused the friction between us and can't imagine the memories he had to deal with, witnessing the expressions on his comrades faces as they died. I'm thankful he doted on you and Lijuan."

"In his own way, he loved you. He did not interact much with YeYe, or NaiNai. They tried to have a relationship with him, but he was jealous of the attention I paid them."

"Did you know the supervisor who reported him to the Red Guard?"

"I met him once. He was a short, heavy man, well over two hundred pounds. Your father had many disagreements with him and argued for restorative justice, maybe because of all the years he had fought the Japanese. I asked him if he had been angry long enough, but he never answered."

"I've made peace with Father. Catherine told me not to dwell on the past, and Julian thought Father might have been conditioned by his war experiences. When Wong located him in prison, we tried to get him out, but the man Wong sent to find him was killed. I feel bad that a man died trying to find him."

We swung for a while in silence. Then she said, "Do you remember the fortune teller's premonitions about you?"

"I do, and I remember telling Lijuan I didn't believe in fortune telling."

"Your NaiNai, the fortune teller, and the holy man all said you had a purpose already written for you."

"And many of their predictions have come true. I was arms and legs for Julian and have been eyes for Catherine. I've had a good life here in Collingwood because of Catherine, Julian, and Caitlin."

"YeYe taught you all music is twelve notes between octaves, and every person experiences those same twelve notes, but how you played them made the difference in your life. I am proud of who you have become and grateful Julian treated you like his own son. I apologize for my earlier comments about Maureen. She is a fine woman, and if Aria looks like Caitlin or Maureen, either would be fine with me."

⁒

When Caitlin and I were alone, she said, "Mum told me she appreciates Kathleen living with her and would like to make it permanent. She thought we could use Kathleen's suite for Lily and Lijuan."

"That's a good thought. I'm sure Maureen's been lonely since your father died."

"Kathleen is taking extra classes to complete her teaching degree, and it's easier to study at Mother's because there aren't so many distractions. I cleaned her room today and noticed she'd moved most of her things out."

"How did you feel about that?"

"Lonely. She's my best friend, and we shared everything with each other."

"Let her know she's always welcome here. In fact, tell them both they can stay with us any time."

"I told Kathleen that's what you'd say, and I'll tell Mum."

⁂

I let Caitlin sleep in Saturday morning and took Aria for a morning walk. I was feeding her canned baby food when Mother came into the kitchen and laughed hysterically, pointing toward the food smeared all over Aria's face.

"My son is a banker, not a mother. Let me feed her so the food enters her mouth and does not miss the opening."

She cleaned Aria's face and was feeding her congee with chopsticks when Caitlin entered the kitchen.

"Mother made congee. Would you like some?" I asked.

"I'm not hungry, just tea."

"Are you feeling okay?"

"Fine."

"Did you sleep well?"

"Not so good."

Mother served congee to everyone, but Caitlin stirred it around the bowl, then pushed it away and said, "Can we talk outside, alone?"

We sat in the backyard by the blue spruce, and she was quiet for a few minutes. "All I hear all day is Mandarin. At first, Lily tried to speak English, but lately, she has spoken and sung in Mandarin to Aria. Chukee's words are Mandarin. And when Wei Lei comes over, we sit at the table together, and they talk in Mandarin, but no one translates. You don't even translate much anymore. It's like living in a foreign country, and now Aria prefers congee to her baby food, and Lily's putting chopsticks in Aria's mouth. I don't know how much more I can take. I expected a period of adjustment and supported your efforts to bring her here. Don't get me wrong. I'm glad to have her, but I can't shake feeling like an outsider in my home. It's only going to get worse when Lijuan arrives." Tears filled her eyes.

I wasn't sure how to respond and took a few moments before I said, "I'm sorry. I've been so absorbed with Mother's transition and work that I neglected to realize how impactful this has been on you. You've gone from spending your days with Aria and Kathleen to watching over a household of Chinese. I've noticed you've been quiet lately and associated it with Aria's teething and sleepless nights. You've lost your privacy and routine. Anyone would be overwhelmed. We can adjust, but I don't believe you're telling me everything that's bothering you. You just lost your father, and you're going through the grieving process. And your best friend is no longer living with us."

"I do miss Daddy, but especially miss Kathleen. Since early childhood, we talked daily about our lives, and now we hardly see each other."

"And yesterday, you saw her empty room."

"The reality of Kathleen leaving really hit me. But she needs a quiet place to study and this certainly isn't a quite house. Besides, Mum likes having her there."

"Maybe you and Aria should visit your Mum and Kathleen more often."

"I try to keep Aria on a schedule, but with so much disruption, her naps have been short and irregular. You've noticed how frequently she wakes up at night. Lily picks her up when she cries, and I can't communicate with her to tell her no. It's all frustrating for me."

"I'll ask Lily not to get Aria from her bed during nap time and remind her to speak more English, especially around Aria. Maybe Wei Lei can help Mother assimilate."

"These are good steps, but you're guilty too. I've noticed you even speak Mandarin to Aria."

"You have my permission to punch me in the ribs when I don't speak English. Then, when I'm all black and blue, I'll tell Mother I'm taking boxing lessons."

She punched me in the ribs and laughed. "There's another thing," she nervously tapped the bench with her finger and looked away from me.

"Please, tell me."

"No more congee for a while."

"I'll prepare oatmeal with berries and walnuts, make waffles, omelets, or French toast, all with Canadian bacon."

"Just toast and coffee today. But the menu variety will be appreciated."

"I was born to be a short-order cook. Anything else?"

"I want to take Aria to visit Mum and Kathleen while you speak to your Mother and call Wei Lei."

"Stay as long as you want, and ask Maureen if she'll keep Aria for a few hours this evening, so I can take you to dinner. We deserve a date night."

"I love you, Winson LeBlanc."

"And you're the love of my life."

Chapter Twelve

Mother had been with us six weeks, and we had nearly given up hope of ever seeing Lijuan when I received a telegram at the bank from Eng:

> **Lijuan arrived. Complications and added expenses $10,000. Reply to Eng at Imperial General Store Vancouver for arrival date. Bring money. –Eng**

I was elated and incensed at the same time. Eng gave me the impression he had conscience and decency. But he was still controlled by the syndicate and withheld $25,000 of Dung's money intended for Chukee's care and now was extorting $10,000 more with this gambit for added expenses. There was no way to verify the costs he was claiming. I immediately called Caitlin and read her the telegram.

"Love, I know it's not right, but calm down and consider what's at stake. You were willing to take Chukee for nothing and received $25,000, and you were also willing to pay to bring your family here, so we're still ahead."

"I feel like reporting Eng operating on D'Arcy Island to the RCMP."

"Haven't you already told Clive and David Yonge about D'Arcy?"

"Yes, but they're bound by attorney-client privilege and can't tell the authorities without my consent. I haven't told Chief Kirkpatrick or Ellen Jerome."

"But will you?"

"Not until I get Lijuan. The trafficking ring is like tar; it sticks on everything it touches."

"When will you be going?"

"I'll rearrange my schedule with Peggy and try getting tickets for tonight's evening train. If I take Mother with me, it'll be a three-day journey each way. I haven't seen Lijuan in eighteen years. We won't recognize each other, but she and Mother should know each other."

"Lily will want to go. Assure me you won't step foot on D'Arcy island?"

"I'll use the $10,000 as negotiating terms to pick her up in Vancouver. Will you pack a bag for Mother and me, two small satchels with minimal clothing?

"Sure. Do you want me to tell Lily?"

"You can try. Mother will understand 'Lijuan' and 'Vancouver' and will see you packing her bag and want to help. But I don't like leaving you alone. Will you ask Rhoda to stay with you until I get home?"

"Sure. Rhoda's here most of the time anyway. I don't know what we'd do without her."

My next call was to David Yonge. He offered to pick us up at the train station and invited us to stay with him. I was hesitant because I didn't know Lijuan's condition, but he suggested we'd be more comfortable with him than in a hotel. When I told him about the $10,000 payment, he suggested I wire $9,800 to his law firm's trust account, which would be available for immediate withdrawal when I arrived, and bring another $500 in cash for the balance and travel expenses.

I sent the following response to Eng:

> **_"Arriving Friday morning. Contact in BC at 263-8443."_**

David gave me permission to use his home phone number as my contact. When I told Mother we had train tickets to pick up Lijuan, she had numerous questions. I asked Kai to take us to the train station to avoid disrupting Aria's schedule.

On the drive, Kai assured me he would help with Chukee and watch over Caitlin and Aria. I was apprehensive about Lijuan, but Mother was elated.

In English, I told Kai, "It's a long trip, and I'm more than a little concerned about meeting the syndicate. When this is over, I'll report them to the police."

Mother must have noticed the concerned expression on my face and said, "Do not worry. With all the uncertainty I have lived with the past eighteen years, I will accept whatever is meant to be and be glad to be reunited with both of my children."

I chose the open-seating car and single berths on the train for the night. We walked from car to car and found seats in the last carriage before the baggage car. Our seats were across from a large woman who squirmed and turned her head away from us. After the train pulled away from the depot, she moved to another seat.

It was a long three-day ride, and neither of us slept much. I wished we had flown. David greeted us at the Vancouver station and took us to his apartment in a downtown high-rise building. We freshened up, and over tea, he said, "Your funds arrived and are available whenever you need them, but I haven't heard from Eng. Maybe you should call."

"The only contact I have is the Imperial General Store. If the bank closes at three, maybe we should withdraw the money today to have it available."

"I'll call my office and have my partner withdraw the cash and put it in our safe. The bank is in the lobby of my office building."

"You're making a difficult situation bearable."

"I'm here to ensure everything goes smoothly. I'll even go with you to pick up Lijuan."

I called the Imperial General Store and was told someone would call in the next few hours. David ordered lunch to be delivered, and we discussed other things while Mother rested. It was almost three o'clock when the phone rang. I was glad we had planned ahead, and the cash was available at David's office.

The caller didn't identify himself or wait for a response. All he said was Imperial tonight, nine o'clock, back door, ring bell, bring money, get girl.

I was relieved we wouldn't be going to an island, but David had concerns about Chinatown. Mother stayed at David's while I went with him to get the money.

He suggested we drive to Imperial General Store and get a sense of the area. He knew Chinatown well and said it wouldn't be safe on the streets at night, so he should drive me. We were both big guys, but the people we were dealing with were probably armed, and we weren't.

"Should I hire protection like a Private Investigator to take me tonight?"

"I have a better idea. I have friends from my military days during WWII. Several of us get together regularly. I'll call them from my office and see if they're willing to help."

"I'll be glad to pay them."

"I doubt they'd take your money. They'll appreciate the excitement."

David dropped me in front of Imperial General Store and drove around the block. When I entered the store, a loud bell signaled my arrival, and the wood floor creaked. I was reminded of Hangzhou, except for the fluorescent fixtures which produced a blue-white light above the long aisles lined with shelves stocked with anything you could ask for: housewares, canned goods, clothing, shoes, and hardware items. Smoke hung in the air and surrounded a thin clerk sitting on a high stool behind a counter at the rear of the store with a direct view of the front door. Behind him was a wall with two wooden swinging doors.

"Welcome." The clerk greeted me in Mandarin. "Need help?"

"Looking for black fungus for a stir fry," I replied in Mandarin.

"We don't carry it. Try Sun Hing's at the end of the block."

I didn't want to hang around too long and be recognized later, so I left, saying thank you on my way out. David picked me up at the end of the block, and we drove to his office. While he contacted his friends, I called Caitlin, and she was overjoyed we would receive Lijuan in Chinatown and not D'Arcy Island.

On the way to David's apartment, he picked up Chinese take-out and it looked like enough to feed an army.

"How many friends did you invite?"

"Only three, but they like to eat. They might get to my apartment before us."

"Lily doesn't know they're coming."

"They know. And Joe speaks Mandarin."

Lily was sitting in the living room with two Chinese men who were drinking beer. A big, broad-shouldered muscular man said, "About time the grub arrived."

"Ross, Joe, thanks for coming. Good to see you entertaining Lily," David made introductions in English.

Ross raised his beer as if giving a toast and said, "At your service."

"Enjoyed the time with Lily. She told me quite a story about her son, so you must be Wen Shun." Joe said.

"It's Winson now. If you spoke Mandarin, you made her day," I said.

He shook my hand and said, "I'm first generation and grew up speaking Mandarin. Your mother is a remarkable woman and reminds me of my mother."

"Where's Benny? I'm hungry. He was born late, and nothing's changed." Ross took the bags of food from me and went to the kitchen with David.

Joe went out on the balcony to smoke while David and Ross set the table. "Joe has quite a background," Mother said.

"Did he tell you about his WWII experiences with David?"

"He spoke of growing up in Chinatown. His parents struggled, so he began earning money when he was eight, delivering the newspapers. Ross added that in high school, Joe shot dice and ran a craps game."

"Dinner is served," Ross said as he put food on the table.

Ross sat next to Mother, and I started to sit on her other side at the head of the table, but Ross shook his head, pointed to the seat across from her, and said, "That's for Joe."

When Joe came in from the balcony, he took the chair at the head of the table. Ross started for the food, but Joe said, "Ross, where are your manners? Let Lily serve herself first."

There was so much banter in English that I couldn't translate for Mother. She sat there looking confused and awkward. Finally, Joe spoke to her in Mandarin, "Please, ladies first, Lily. I'm trying to get these good-for-nothings to be gentlemen, and it's near impossible."

Benny arrived late carrying a bakery box. "Sorry I'm late, but I knew Joe wouldn't be happy unless we had his sweets."

While we were eating, David spoke about how they joined the military together and had to depend on each other to survive brutal conditions fighting the Japanese in the Borneo jungles. They put their lives on the line daily, working undercover, unshaven, and dressed like mercenaries. Joe was obviously the leader, and these men looked up to him.

After dinner, we set about making plans for the evening, and Joe was chosen to drive Mother and me. Ross was the biggest of the group, looked the most intimidating, and would ride along to protect the money while Mother and I identified Lijuan.

Benny would drive David in a second car and wait a short distance away in case of trouble. We had confirmed a payphone was on the corner in case they needed to call the police.

Mother listened to our plans, but I don't think she understood much and didn't ask any questions. The six of us departed from David's home at quarter to nine, the men dressed in black slacks and dark jackets. I noticed at least three of them carried pistols and heard them talk of heavier weaponry.

We drove through Gastown and knew we had arrived in Chinatown when car after car lined the curbs, streets teamed with festivities, and there was the buzz of neon signs for Canton Gardens, Ming's Chop Suey, Pender Café, and the Bamboo Terrace. I was looking at the throng of people when Joe slammed on the brakes to stop from hitting the car in front of us, and two pistols slid from under the front seats and hit my foot, landing on the floorboard between us. Mother grasped my arm, closed her eyes, and looked away.

"Just push them babies back under the seat," Ross said.

"Are Benny and David armed too?" I asked.

"They have the heavier guns. We're not taking any chances. It's like we're back in Borneo," he laughed like this was a joy ride.

We were stopped in traffic for several minutes, and I asked Joe, "What's going on? Can we get around this bottleneck? We're going to be late."

"Street's blocked. Could be any number of things, an accident, construction, or a gang fight!"

"Is there anything you can do?" I didn't want to miss our appointment and lose the chance to receive Lijuan.

"I'm going to be creative. I grew up in Chinatown and know my way around." He put his hand out the window and motioned Benny to back up so we could make a U-turn. Benny and David followed.

He drove us through several dark alleys with few people and lots of trash. My heart pounded in my chest as we stopped at the back door of Imperial General Store. I was in the rear seat passenger side and Mother sat beside me.

"Stay in the car while I ring the doorbell," I said to Mother.

She grabbed my arm as I opened the door, and I said, "I'll be careful."

My heart raced as I approached the door. "Please, God, keep everyone safe," I prayed to myself as I pressed the bell. It was 9:08 by my watch. When no one opened the door, I pressed the bell again.

The door finally opened a crack, and an old man peeked out and said in Mandarin, "You are late. Now you wait." He closed the door, and I heard it lock.

The alley was dark, with few cars and lots of garbage bins. I could see David and Benny at the end of the road. Benny's car was old and looked like it belonged in the area.

When the door opened again, a muscular young man with a thin black mustache extending from under his nose, past the corners of his mouth, and several inches beyond his chin said, "Tao Wen Shun?" A thin cigarette wobbled out of the side of his mouth.

"Yes."

"Why you bring so many people?" He looked toward Joe and Ross.

"They are local Chinese friends with a car to bring me here."

"You have money?"

"You'll get the money when I see my sister."

"She is here but not awake."

"What do you mean?"

"She is sedated."

I was ready to push down the door, but I knew that wouldn't help. "Take my mother and me to her." I waved to Mother to step out of the car.

"Money first, and we bring girl to you."

""You'll get the money when I see my sister." I motioned for Mother to get back in the car.

"Just mother come in."

"I'm coming with her. You can see she's too small to carry my sister if she is drugged."

"I take mother to sister. You wait here with money."

I spoke to Mother in Mandarin, and she took hold of my arm and said, "I am getting my daughter. I will be okay."

"You identify her and come back outside. If Lijuan is in there, I'll give this man the money he wants."

When she went inside, the lock clicked on the door behind her, and I paced back and forth, but Ross told me to wait in the car, so we wouldn't attract attention. Each minute seemed like an eternity, and I couldn't sit still.

The back door of the store opened, and I jumped out of the car and went to Mother. She stood in the doorway, pale as a ghost.

"Is it Lijuan?"

"I spoke to her, but she did not answer."

"Mother," I took hold of her arms, looked her in the eyes, and said as calmly as possible, "Tell me, is it Lijuan?"

"It has been eighteen years." Mother put her hands on the side of her face, "She has the same birthmark on her forearm, but otherwise, I would not know her. She is my daughter but is not herself, and Zhang is with her."

Suddenly Zhang appeared behind Mother, a cigar stub wedged in the crook of his mouth and yellow sweat stains under the sleeves of his khaki shirt. He narrowed his eyes, removed the stub with his thumb and forefinger, and said with a menacing grin, "So, I see you again."

Mother recoiled and took a half-step toward me. I put myself between her and Zhang, and we stared at each other. One minute, two, another went by, and his eyes started blinking rapidly, and he fidgeted, but neither of us said a word. Finally, he said, "Speak."

"I'm taking my sister, Lijuan. Bring her outside, and I'll give you the money."

"She is a wild one. Wants to go back to China. Drugs only way to keep her calm. You have your hands full with this one."

I was ready to barge through him and the door to get my sister, but I didn't know who was behind Zhang or inside. "I want to see her now."

"Mother has seen her. Money first."

I opened the car door and asked Ross to show Zhang the money. He pulled the satchel from between his legs and showed the cash.

Zhang motioned to the young man with the mustache and said, "Count the cash."

The man walked toward the car, looking back and forth down the alley. When I saw a revolver in Joe's hand, I pushed Mother behind me and looked toward the end of the block where Benny and David watched. The man blocked my sight of Ross as he counted the cash.

"$10,000," the man said.

When Ross closed the satchel, I told Mother to get in the car. When she started to say something, I squeezed her arm hard, and Ross held the door open for her.

"Now get my sister."

"I need $5,000 more," Zhang said.

"You're getting the money Eng asked for."

"It's me you deal with now, and I have what you want."

"I don't have any more money."

"You have money. I am told you own a bank."

He treated me like I was the scared teenager back in Hangzhou, hiding behind my mother in his store. I thought about what Julian and YeYe would do next and said, "We're done!"

I got in the car, and Mother gasped.

"Joe, let's go," I said.

Before I closed the car door, I heard, "I'll bring her out," and Zhang returned to the store with his friend.

Five minutes seemed like forever as we waited, but the door finally opened, and Zhang had Lijuan in his arms, and his muscle man was behind him with a sawed-off shotgun. Lijuan hung like a limp towel, and I hoped we could revive her as I took her from him.

"Give him the money and let's get out of here," I said to Ross as I gently placed Lijuan on the back seat between us, so we could hold her up.

Ross held a gun in his hand as he handed the satchel to Zhang. I was praying no one would shoot.

When the backdoor to Imperial General Store closed, Joe pulled the car away slowly, and we headed to David's apartment, and David and Benny followed.

We were fortunate not to have more conflict at the exchange, but we still had the problem of Lijuan's condition. We couldn't take her to a hospital because she was illegal. In the parking garage at David's building, David said he would hold an elevator for us. If we all were in one elevator, no one else could get in. Ross and I got in first and held Lijuan upright between us. She didn't make a sound, and Mother kept saying her name.

When we entered David's apartment, I put Lijuan in a guest room with Mother and closed the door.

There weren't enough words to express my appreciation for these men. They risked their lives for a total stranger, and I was humbled by their willingness to help. When I tried to thank them, Joe said they were happy to help, and Ross said they hadn't had that much fun in a long time. The men said their goodbyes and wished me the best with Lijuan.

"I'm going to make a phone call. She obviously needs a doctor. I have a friend who will come here." David excused himself, and I went into the room to check on Lijuan.

Mother had a damp cloth and was pressing it on her forehead, cheeks, and neck. "We need to wake her up," she said.

"I'll make a strong tea and see if we can get her to swallow. Are you sure this is Lijuan? I don't recognize her."

When Mother lifted the sleeve on her right arm, revealing a half-inch birthmark, I immediately recognized it.

"Keep talking to her like you did in the car."

By the time the doctor arrived, she had moaned a few times but didn't open her eyes. While the doctor examined her with Mother in the room, I had a few minutes to call Caitlin and let her know we were safe and had Lijuan, but she was unconscious. She expressed concern for Lijuan's condition but was relieved we were safe.

David entered the room and handed me a cup of hot tea as I hung up the phone. "It's going to be a long night. You're going to need this. She's not in any condition to travel. You're welcome to stay here as long as necessary."

"You're a true friend, and I hate to impose on you."

"You're not imposing. Let's take this one day at a time."

"You've done so much for us already."

We sat in silence for a few minutes. Lost in thought for my sister and her medical condition, I didn't hear Dr. Cohen enter the room.

"Your sister is starting to come around. She was heavily sedated. Any idea what drug?"

"My guess would be opium. The Chinese seem to have an unending supply. Will she be okay?"

"I can't answer that. It depends on if she's addicted or overdosed. She should be hospitalized, but David shared your circumstances with me. She's agitated, so I left the room to see if your mother can calm her. I don't want to medicate her, not knowing what's in her system. If you go in and talk to her, it might help."

I was at Lijuan's bedside in a matter of seconds. Her bloodshot eyes were open, unfocused, and looked wild with fury. Mother sang a Chinese lullaby but stopped when I knelt beside Lijuan.

I tried to hold her hand, but she pulled away. "Lijuan, I'm Wen Shun, your brother. You're safe with Mother and me."

She didn't respond but turned her head to look at me. I wore YeYe's ivory medallion around my neck, which caught her eye. She reached out her hand, and I lifted the medallion over my head and held it before her. The anger in her eyes subdued as she clasped the ivory in her hand. Her first words were "YeYe."

She looked from me to Mother and back to me.

"It's YeYe's medallion. Do you remember he gave it to me when I left Hangzhou?"

She didn't answer but closed her eyes and pressed the medallion against her cheek. Mother started singing to her again. I knelt and prayed God would restore her to us.

Dr. Cohen came in a few minutes later. "This will be a tough night for her. Try to keep her awake, keep her drinking fluids, and maybe a little soup. She appears to be dehydrated, along with the effects of the drugs. David is warming chicken broth. Give it to her by tiny sips and not too much at once."

"What are her chances?"

"That's up to her, but she's with family now, which is her best likelihood to respond. We don't know what she's been through. Physically she may be okay, but she may have psychological issues. I didn't notice any needle marks on her arms, so hopefully, she's not addicted to the drugs."

"She's always been strong and determined. Whatever issues she has, we'll help her through it."

"I can see that. I live in the building. If you need me tonight, have David call. Regardless, I'll return in the morning and check on her."

"Dr. Cohen, we can't thank you enough."

Mother and I propped her on pillows and took turns sitting with her, feeding her broth. She didn't want it at first but eventually quit fighting. She didn't let go of the medallion. At about two in the morning, she indicated to Mother she needed to urinate. I'd helped Chukee and Julian and knew what to do, but I also wanted her to have privacy. I lifted her to a sitting position and turned her body so her legs could dangle over the side of the bed. I held her in place for several minutes.

"Lijuan, can you stand on your feet?" I asked.

She gave a slight nod.

I had Mother sit on one side of her, and I sat on the other. I placed my arm around her back and gently lifted her. Mother rose at the same time, bearing part of Lijuan's weight. We stood for a minute, and she tried to take a step forward. Slowly we made our way to the bathroom. I didn't want to embarrass Lijuan or Mother, so I lifted the toilet seat lid and positioned Lijuan in front of it. It was a small bathroom with a wall three feet in front of the commode. I placed Lijuan's hands on the wall for balance and turned my back.

"It's okay to leave us. I'm strong enough to help her, and these toilets are easy to use," Mother said.

After we returned her to bed, I made Mother rest on the other twin bed.

I sat in a chair next to Lijuan and talked to her about growing up together. She had a blank look most of the time, but occasionally I said something which elicited awareness in her eyes.

At about five in the morning, Mother woke and told me to sleep a little. She was softly singing to Lijuan as I dozed off. I heard David in the kitchen a few hours later and joined him. The coffee was already percolating.

"Winson, I'm not a cook, but I manage. Are you ready for breakfast? I can make congee in a pressure cooker. It'll be ready in about twenty minutes."

"Coffee smells wonderful, and I could use a cup to wake up. I've always made congee on the stovetop, which takes hours."

Dr. Cohen arrived about the time the congee was ready. He didn't know what it was. After he took a taste, he said it was perfect to feed Lijuan, but to add a bit of cool chicken broth.

I sat at the table with David, savoring my coffee, while Dr. Cohen checked on Lijuan. When he returned to the kitchen, he said she'd improved since last night, her heart rate was almost normal, and her blood pressure was lower, yet still too high. These were normal reactions to an overdose of sedative drugs.

"She's still not talking, but she did say 'YeYe,' which is our grandfather. I was wearing his medallion, and when she saw it around my neck, she wanted it."

"I saw it in her hand. Did it calm her?"

"At first, it did, but she still gets agitated. Mother's singing seemed to soothe her, and I told her stories from our childhood, hoping she'd remember."

"Did you and your mother get any sleep?"

"We both napped for a couple of hours. Can we take her to Collingwood soon?"

"She's in no condition to travel, probably not for several weeks."

"You can stay as long as needed," David said.

"I hope it won't be that long. We both have responsibilities to tend to. Thank you for examining her, Dr. Cohen."

"After you feed her, see if you can give her a shower or bath, which might make her more alert. I'll be back in the afternoon."

Mother was delighted to see the congee. She would eat a spoonful and then feed one to Lijuan. David brought hot tea for Mother, which she also shared with Lijuan once it cooled. Lijuan was shaky, and we didn't trust her with a cup. A partial smile appeared when I asked her if she would like a bath.

I suggested Mother shower with her, but Lijuan shook her head no. So I ran a bath and asked Mother to be in the room with her. Lijuan's clothes were dirty and tattered, and she had an offensive odor. Caitlin had packed warmups she thought we could put on Lijuan. She also packed an extra nightgown and light robe. My wife was thoughtful, and I could always count on her to plan ahead.

Mother sat on the commode and talked while Lijuan soaked in the bathtub until Mother finally pulled the plug to drain the water. Lijuan had little strength but could hold the faucets and pull herself up. She was shivering by the time Mother wrapped her in a towel. In the meantime, David gave me a clean set of sheets, and I changed her bed. David was going to wash her clothes with the sheets, but I told him to throw the clothes away.

By the time Dr. Cohen returned, both Lijuan and Mother were sleeping.

"I hardly recognized her with clean clothes and washed hair. Her blood pressure and pulse have improved. Has she talked yet?" Dr. Cohen asked.

"No, but she ate congee and stayed in the bath for a long time. She's been sleeping for about an hour. I'd like to take her back to Collingwood tomorrow if you think she can make the trip?"

"It's risky. Definitely not by public transportation in her condition. The good news is she's not shown withdrawal symptoms from the narcotics, indicating she's not addicted. The fact she's not talking suggests she's in shock. It must have been a very traumatic journey for her."

"I don't know anything about her trip here other than it was by ship. My mother's passage was extremely difficult, and she was raped numerous times by the man who escorted her. Maybe the same thing happened to Lijuan."

"I haven't examined her that way. I didn't want to be intrusive. Your mother showed me bruises on Lijuan's body. They're superficial, but she was definitely roughed up some. I would suggest we watch her for a few more days before you move her."

When he left, David said, "Joe's retired and has cousins in Toronto. I'll ask him if he would be willing to drive you home. I would do it, but I have business here I must tend to."

"Would he drive us all that way?"

"Driving is therapeutic for Joe. He takes several long trips a year and loves driving cross country, so he'll jump at the chance. You won't have to stop for the night with both of you driving. The transcontinental highway is almost complete, so you can make the trip in forty-eight to fifty hours, depending on how many times you stop, weather conditions, and construction."

"If Joe is willing, I'd like to leave tomorrow or Monday, with Dr. Cohen's okay."

"You need sleep before you go. You've had less than two hours in the last two days. So I'll call Joe while you take a nap."

"Wake me in two hours or sooner if you need me."

I awoke to screaming and rushed into Lijuan's room. Mother had her arms wrapped around a sobbing Lijuan. She finally stopped crying when Mother sang, and she allowed Mother to continue holding her.

"I'd like to call Caitlin before it gets too late. Are you okay staying with her for a few more minutes?"

"I can take care of my baby. You call Caitlin," Mother said.

"Baby," Lijuan repeated.

"Yes, you'll always be my baby," Mother said.

"My baby," Lijuan repeated with agitation in her voice.

"Yes, you are my baby, Lijuan," Mother cooed.

"No, my baby," Lijuan screamed and pounded her fists on Mother.

I stepped in and grabbed her hands so she wouldn't injure Mother. She fought me, but I held on to her firmly and softly said, "Lijuan, you're safe with Mother and Wen Shun." I tried to relax my grip on her, but she fought hard for several minutes and eventually calmed. I wondered if she had left a baby in China, but I didn't want to ask and agitate her more.

We eventually got her up, walked her around the apartment, and brought her to the dining table for dinner. She ate a little rice with chopsticks and sipped tea but didn't smile or interact with us, even though we all tried. After dinner, Mother took her back into the bedroom while I helped David clean up.

"Joe's willing to drive you and is coming over this evening to make plans. Do you have money for the trip?"

"I have a Chargex credit card and checkbook, but not much cash."

"Unfortunately, you may have trouble getting places to accept a credit card or check from a Chinaman. I have a couple hundred in cash, but you may need more. Why don't you wait until Monday when I can cash a $500 check for you? Then, Lijuan will have another day to get stronger, and you'll have plenty of cash for the trip.

By Sunday, Lijuan's condition was much improved. Her blood pressure and heart rate were normal, and she ate small amounts and fed herself. Dr. Cohen wasn't happy about us leaving so soon but understood my need to get home.

When I told him about her reaction to the word 'baby,' he asked if we'd noticed her lactating.

"My wife is nursing our eight-month-old daughter, and when it's time to feed, she starts leaking, but I've not noticed that with Lijuan."

"She's frail and small-boned. If she had a baby and stopped nursing, she would dry up in a few weeks. Leaving a child behind would certainly have added to her trauma."

"Do you think she might overreact when she sees my daughter?"

"She might. Maybe you should carefully plan such a meeting."

"Thank you. I'd like to pay you for taking care of Lijuan."

"David is a good friend and has helped me many times. I was glad to be able to help and won't take your money. Safe travels, and call me if you need anything." He gave me his card.

I was overwhelmed by all the kindness I received from David and his friends.

I called Caitlin to let her know we were driving home on Monday and to expect us by Wednesday evening. She told me Rhoda had taken Chukee to her house because she was worried about all the activity in our house with Lijuan coming. Chukee was my responsibility, but I appreciated how Rhoda cared for him and knew he was in good hands. It was always difficult for me to accept help from others.

⁂

We left David's house in the dark at six in the morning. Joe drove five hours in light rain and stopped for gas and the loo in Kamloops. I drove the second shift in heavier rain while Joe took a nap. By the time we reached Canyon Hot Springs, Joe woke up. We were in the mountains, and the rain had turned into a Spring snowstorm. Mother and Lijuan were sleeping, bundled in blankets. It'd been a long and tiring day, and Joe suggested he drive and for me to rest. I awoke suddenly when I heard brakes screeching. We slid to a stop along the shoulder and barely avoided hitting the car in front of us.

"That was close. Fortunately, the snow hasn't turned to ice, so we didn't skid out of control. There must be an accident or obstruction ahead," Joe said.

I rolled down the window, and snow blew in from strong winds, so I immediately closed it. Joe said we were about ninety miles west of Lake Louise and had nearly half a tank of gas. There wasn't much to do but wait. Because of the freezing temperature, Joe didn't turn off the engine.

Lijuan was asleep, and Mother asked what had happened. After about thirty minutes, Joe pulled out a cigarette, twirled it between his fingers, then stuck it in his mouth and said, "I don't like it when I'm confined and can't keep moving." He tapped the steering wheel, squirmed in his seat for a while, then said, "I'm going to walk ahead and see if I can discover the problem."

As he walked away into the darkness, I closed my eyes and thought of Joe being air-dropped behind enemy lines in Borneo and Mother being taken into the mountains, both facing unknown and uncertain futures. I don't know how long I was asleep when the driver's door opened. Joe brushed the snow off his coat, closed the door, and said, "I spoke to a trucker with a CB radio. He said an eighteen-wheeler jackknifed and a tow truck is clearing the highway now. We should be good to go soon. Were you worried?"

"Not a bit. As long as we weren't behind enemy lines in Borneo, and you're behind the wheel, I'm good."

He grinned and said, "David can't keep his mouth shut about Borneo." He laughed so hard he woke Lijuan, then rubbed his hands together and asked for coffee."

Joe was a natural leader, and I wanted to ask him about serving in the jungles of Borneo, but after his comment about David, I didn't.

The journey took us fifty-two hours, and the last six hours were in heavy rain. Joe and I were both exhausted when we pulled into my driveway on Wednesday evening.

Aria was in bed for the night, and Caitlin had tea and soup waiting for us. Mother thanked her but said she would like to take Lijuan upstairs and let her have a long bath. Caitlin had moved Mother into the suite that had been ours when we first married and then Kathleen's. Mother noticed the small kitchen area Julian had built for us.

I offered Joe a glass of McCallan, and he quickly said, "I'll take it neat."

Chapter Thirteen

Early in the morning, I had coffee with Joe before he left, then went into the nursery to spend time with Aria. She kicked her feet and squealed when she saw me. When I took her into the bedroom for Caitlin to nurse, Caitlin said, "Your sister looked like a frightened kitten last night. How are we going to introduce her to Aria?"

"I don't know what to do. Mother said she would tell her about Aria before they came down this morning. I heard them walking upstairs and heard no screaming so maybe that's good news."

I went upstairs to check on them while Caitlin fed Aria cereal and bananas in the kitchen. Lijuan had a quiet night and enjoyed the bath, but Mother didn't tell her about Aria and thought they should stay in their room today. We were both careful not to say the word baby, but there would be a time when Lijuan would hear Aria, and we had to be ready for her reaction.

When I returned downstairs, I called Peggy at the bank, and when I hung up, Caitlin was carrying Aria into my office.

"What are you doing this morning?" Caitlin asked.

"I'll call Bitsy and see if she would be willing to see Lijuan today. Maybe she'll have several ideas."

"But Lijuan doesn't understand English. Wei Lei offered to come over this morning and said she could translate if you need to go to the bank."

'That's good of Wei Lei. I talked to Peggy and told her I was staying home today. I want to be here when Lijuan meets Aria. We can't postpone the inevitable."

Bitsy arrived when Caitlin was putting Aria down for her morning nap. We talked for a few minutes in the parlor, and I told her as much as I knew about Lijuan's life and her reaction to the word baby. Bitsy thought she was driven beyond her normal physical and emotional boundaries and, undoubtedly, past her ability to tolerate abusive treatment."

"We've been trying to love her but don't know how to handle her violent reactions. I feel like I can't leave her and want to protect Caitlin, Mother, and Aria from her outbursts."

"When I first treated war veterans, when one of them heard an explosive sound, he was re-experiencing what happened but not necessarily remembering what happened. The body remembers how it reacted when it heard a particular sound or a certain smell, and it wants to react like it did in the original situation. It's called shell shock. A colleague suggested I put several veterans together in a group, and let them talk among themselves to find their way through their issues by sharing with others who had gone through similar experiences. Maybe that'd help Lijuan."

"I've been through difficult circumstances and would gladly share them with her, but I'm not sure she knows who I am. Sometimes she knows Mother, and other times not."

"It's not intentional she doesn't recognize the past with you; it's just not accessible to her right now. The memory is still there in her brain. She may not remember anything about your time together until she has a flashback. And you're a grown man who is much different than when you were a young brother to your little sister. Her recollection, if it does happen, will be a gradual releasing by the brain."

"She knows YeYe's medallion."

"I noticed you're not wearing it."

"She has it around her neck. It seems to be a comfort for her."

I took Bitsy to the suite and knocked on the door before entering. Mother and Lijuan were sitting on the sofa, and I introduced Bitsy, translating back and forth. Lijuan sat with a blank stare on her face. We only stayed in the room a short time, and when we were in the hallway, Bitsy said, "It's good she's eating and tending to her physical needs, and she smells like she had a nice lavender bath."

"She enjoys the bathtub and had a bath last night when we returned from our road trip. In Vancouver, she woke up screaming from nightmares, but I didn't hear her last night. What do you think?"

"She's in traumatic shock. It'll be difficult for me to counsel her with the language barrier. Normally counseling is done one on one."

"Do you have any suggestions?"

"You were the victim of human trafficking. Do you know any female victims? Their circumstances and experiences are usually different than boys or men."

"Wei Lei's friend, Lysa Wu. She was involved in Dung's organization and forced into prostitution. She has moved away but was willing to return here to testify against Dung."

"Clive said Dung and Tak are dead. Would she consider talking to Lijuan?"

"Wei Lei is in contact with her. I'll ask her if you think it'll help."

"There are no guarantees, but I've successfully put together small groups to deal with trauma. Victims are more willing to share their experiences with other victims."

"I'll call Wei Lei. What about introducing Lijuan to Aria? I told you how she reacts to the word baby."

"I would like to be here when she meets Aria. Do you want to do it today?"

"Both Caitlin and I would rather it happen when I'm home, so today would be good." I looked at my watch and said, "She'll be awake in about thirty minutes. Let's go in the kitchen, talk to Caitlin, and discuss a plan."

After talking to Caitlin, the three of us decided to bring Lijuan downstairs and take her into the parlor where the playpen was to see how she reacted before exposing Aria to her. Once she remained calm, Caitlin would bring Aria in. In the meantime, Caitlin would wake Aria from her nap and feed her so she wouldn't be fussy.

I went upstairs and brought Mother and Lijuan down. Mother was hesitant, but I assured her it was better to introduce Aria while Bitsy was with us and I was home. As we entered the parlor, she looked at the playpen and didn't react. When Bitsy, Mother, Lijuan, and I were seated, I said in Mandarin, "Caitlin is feeding the baby."

Lijuan's eyes brightened, and she said, "Baby" in Mandarin.

"Lijuan, Caitlin and I have a baby."

"My baby!" she said.

"No. Wen Shun and Caitlin's baby," I said.

She looked at me like she didn't understand, but she wasn't agitated. We were making progress.

"Would you like to meet Wen Shun's baby?" Mother asked.

"My baby," she repeated.

"No, Lijuan. Wen Shun's baby." She pointed at me. "Her name is Aria."

I looked at Bitsy, explained what was said, and she nodded to proceed with our plan. I left the room and entered the nursery, where Caitlin was changing Aria. "Bitsy is ready for us to bring Aria into the parlor."

"This is our precious little girl. Are you sure it's okay?"

"No, but we should try while Bitsy's here. She didn't overreact when I said we have a baby, and her name is Aria."

Caitlin lifted Aria into my arms and followed me into the parlor. I heard her say, "Please, God, help us," as we entered the room.

Lijuan immediately stood up and walked toward me with outstretched arms. Of course, Aria clung to me tighter and turned her head away from Lijuan.

"Her name is Aria, and she's eight months old. You're her Auntie Lijuan," I said to Lijuan, who tried to take Aria from my arms, but Caitlin reached up to stop her, and she slapped Caitlin across her face.

Caitlin put her hand up to her cheek and backed away. Aria clung tight to me while Mother and Bitsy jumped up and restrained Lijuan, pulling her toward the sofa. Lijuan wanted no part of it. "My baby," she screamed as she tried to pull away.

Caitlin's eyes welled with tears, her cheek was red, and she bit her lower lip. My wife and sister were both hurting. Mother and Bitsy held Lijuan while she screamed, and Aria shrieked. Pain was etched on everyone's face.

"Are you okay?" I asked Caitlin as I comforted Aria in my arms.

"No. Give her to me. I'm taking her to her room."

When I put Aria in Caitlin's arms, I said, "Please, let me carry Aria to Lijuan one more time. I'll protect her. You have my word. Or you can do it, and I'll be next to you."

She paced back and forth a few times and said, "I know you'll protect her, but I'm frightened. Look what she did to me." Then, she turned to Bitsy, "What do you think?"

"I don't think she'll hurt Aria. She feels Aria's her baby. So let him try one more time."

When Lijuan calmed, I knelt before her, and Aria spotted YeYe's pendant around her neck. Aria reached for the pendant, and Lijuan smiled.

I let Aria touch the medallion, and Lijuan put her hand on Aria's cheek with Mother's help. Mother softly sang a lullaby, and I relaxed a little when Lijuan sang with Mother. Aria touched Lijuan's lips, and a radiant smile spread across Lijuan's face. Mother and Bitsy let go of Lijuan, and she wrapped her arms around Aria and continued singing, but I didn't let go of Aria.

When Aria started wriggling, I said, "Lijuan, don't hold her so tight."

She squeezed Aria even harder, and Aria shrieked. "Lijuan, not so tight, or I'll take her away from you."

"No!" she yelled. "My baby."

Mother said to Lijuan, "Let go of Aria."

Lijuan struggled as Bitsy and Mother grabbed her arms again, and I pulled Aria away and gave her to Caitlin, who took her back to the nursery. Lijuan screamed and tried to go after Caitlin, but I restrained her from behind and lifted her off the ground as she swung her arms and legs in the air.

Mother tried to reason with her, but Lijuan wouldn't listen. The chaos made it difficult to concentrate.

"I didn't understand Lijuan's words, but I can tell from her actions she thinks Aria is her baby," Bitsy said.

"That's exactly what she said."

"You and Lily are going to have to convince her otherwise. I don't think she'll hurt Aria, but she may hurt Caitlin."

I brought my sister into our home, and she was a danger to my wife and daughter. Mother wanted to know what Bitsy said, but I didn't want to translate for Mother in front of Lijuan. "What do we do next?" I asked Bitsy.

"Keep talking to Lijuan and telling her the baby's name is Aria and belongs to you and Caitlin. We may have to get a mild sedative for her."

"She was drugged to get her to Canada. I don't want to give her medications unless there's no other option."

"Then you need to separate Lijuan from Aria for a while."

"Where would I take Lijuan? She doesn't speak or understand English, and this is Caitlin and Aria's home, our home."

"Right now, they need to be separated. The easiest short-term solution is for Caitlin and Aria to temporarily leave. What other choice do you have?"

"Mother can't handle Lijuan when she's like this. I'm going to take her upstairs. Would you talk to Caitlin in the nursery?"

After Bitsy left the room, Mother and I took Lijuan to their room.

My heart broke when I returned to the parlor and found Bitsy alone. Caitlin had packed a few clothes and left for her mother's house with Aria.

"I don't want to do this to my wife and daughter. I should put them first, but what do I do with my sister?"

"This is a shock for Caitlin, but she'll be okay. She realizes your sister has nowhere else to go. Keep talking to Lijuan about her baby and reminding her Aria is your baby. Let's call Wei Lei's friend."

∽

When I arrived at Maureen's a few hours later, Caitlin was alone, and her eyes were red and swollen. She talked about wanting our lives back, and I promised the situation was temporary, hopefully only for a few days. I told her about Lysa's willingness to help Lijuan, and she agreed to drive with me to Toronto on Saturday to pick up Lysa. When it was time to leave, I didn't want to let go of Caitlin.

On the way home, I stopped to see Rhoda and check on Chukee. Rhoda greeted me at the door with a big smile.

"Thank you for moving Chukee here. Our house has been in turmoil since Lijuan arrived."

"I know. Caitlin called and told me what happened today. It's not good that she's staying with her mother."

"I know. Caitlin and I are driving to Toronto on Saturday to pick up Lysa Wu. Bitsy hopes she can help Lijuan since she speaks Mandarin and was forced into prostitution at a young age."

"I'll pray Lijuan improves quickly so Caitlin and Aria can come home where they belong. It's not good for you to be apart."

"We need all the prayers we can get."

When I returned home, Kai made a Chinese dinner and Wei Lei visited with Mother and Lijuan at the kitchen table.

I was thankful for their company and said to Kai, "I didn't know you could cook!"

"I'm full of surprises these days. As you know, life changes with a child on the way, so I've been reflecting on my life. The only thing I knew how to do in China was working in the fields and tending the animals. But cooking with Wei Lei gives me pleasure, and she's a good teacher."

Only Mandarin was spoken at the table, and dinner was served with chopsticks. Lijuan picked at her food and sipped tea. Both Kai and Wei Lei tried to engage her in conversation. Kai asked her about the medallion around her neck, even though he knew it was mine. She reached up, touched it, and said, "YeYe."

"When did you last see YeYe?" Wei Lei asked.

Lijuan shook her head, and tears filled her eyes, "YeYe is dead, and my babies are gone."

Mother put an arm around her and said, "We are here with you and want to help."

"We've missed you, Lijuan, and are glad you're here with us," I said.

She bowed her head and held onto the medallion, and I had a glimmer of hope from hearing her talk.

When I complimented Kai on the meal, he said, "I want more out of life now that I'm going to be a father. I should have been more willing to learn English, but I'll never speak as well as you."

"To get more out of life, you must be open to change. We had a rough start at the logging camp and here in Collingwood. No one would hire us after we arrived. If it wasn't for Jackson's church feeding us and giving us a place to sleep, we could've starved or frozen to death."

"When they called us Yellow, it was a word filled with hate, and it felt like the whole country was against us. You said we had to wear two faces. One we showed to the outside world, and the other was ours. But you insisted we maintain hope and things would change, and you pursued opportunities to improve your life."

"You wanted to go back to China, but I took Mother's advice and looked to the future in Canada."

"When I said goodbye to my mother at the dock in Hangzhou, she didn't say much. I knew she didn't want me to leave China, but she also thought sending me to Canada was the best decision for my future."

"I didn't want Wen Shun to leave either," Mother said. Then she added, "I didn't want to leave Lijuan when the Red Guard took me away."

Lijuan appeared to be listening to our conversation but didn't participate.

"I was scared when I boarded the ship, but after I became friends with Wen Shun, I knew I'd be okay, and look at where we are today," Kai said.

"How do you see your future?" I asked.

"Wei Lei and her mother are both great cooks. They're willing to teach me, and we've been discussing opening a Chinese restaurant since there isn't one in town, but it will need to wait until our child is born. Wei Lei's parents want to return to Collingwood to help us."

"I know a banker who might be willing to provide a loan to get you started."

∽

Wei Lei was at the back door by 7:30 the next morning to spend the day with Mother and Lijuan. She greeted me and said, "Kai is fixing breakfast for everyone at the Lawrence house and said for you to join them."

"You're training is doing him plenty of good, and I'm serious about supporting you in a restaurant. Dinner was delicious last night."

"It was good quality, and he's improving his skills. This baby has him looking for a better future for us. Thank you for encouraging him."

"We're family, and that's what we do."

"Are Lily and Lijuan still asleep?"

"I heard them stirring."

"You go, and I'll make them breakfast."

When I arrived at the bank, I called Catherine before tending to business, told her about Lijuan and asked for her advice.

"Does she like music?"

"YeYe crafted musical instruments, Mother and I played them, and she loved to sing along. She grew up with music in the house, and was always happy during those times."

"Music is sound, and sound is vibrations in your ear. The ear translates the vibration into electrical signals to the brain. Understand that parts of the brain need to connect. From what you've told me, there's been a break in Lijuan's synapsis caused by how she was treated and the environment she was forced to be part of for a prolonged period. It was similar to your father's war experiences. Play music with repetitive scores in the house. Try it every day for a week."

"How did you discover this concept?"

"When struggling with my blindness, I would sit in the garden near a beehive. I liked to hear the bees, but then I discovered I liked the sound crickets made. Each sound triggered a different emotion. I spoke to my music professor, who told me about what repetitive sound does to the brain." She paused for a few moments. "Winson, from your silence, you must think this is strange advice."

"Nothing you say surprises me."

"What your sister has experienced is abnormal, so you must consider nonstandard remedies, or you may never see the sister you and your mother once knew."

"That makes sense, but I need it to happen quickly because Caitlin and Aria belong home."

"Be patient. One day the flower that's your sister will bloom. In the meantime, tell Caitlin to bring Aria to spend time with us. We'll love on them. Aria changes so much every time we see her."

"That's exactly how I'm feeling, and I don't want to miss a single day. Aria's crawling and trying to pull herself up to stand. She cut two teeth while I was in Vancouver. I apologize for always sharing my problems with you."

"No apology necessary. Remember, a joy shared doubles the joy, and a sorrow shared, halves the sorrow."

∞

I called Wei Lei and suggested she play one of Julian's records when Lijuan was downstairs, and I gave her the name of an album with repetitive rhythms. I struggled to concentrate on bank business and went to see Caitlin at lunch. I could hardly wait to put my arms around my wife and daughter. I missed them both so much.

Caitlin said sleep was difficult because Aria didn't have her own bed and kept Caitlin up most of the night. She didn't like changing Aria's routine.

She asked about Lijuan, and I told her about my conversation with Catherine and asked Wei Lei to play music in the house. I saw the stress on Caitlin's face, unlike any I had seen before. Our time apart was difficult for both of us.

I was fulfilling an implied vow to provide for Mother and Lijuan. They didn't choose to come to Canada, and I was thankful Mother's arrival was smooth, but Lijuan's behavior was unexpected, and the family strain and disruption couldn't continue without unintended consequences. Like Caitlin, I hoped the situation was temporary.

On my way back to the bank, I stopped to check on everyone at home, but no one was there. I hoped they had taken Lijuan for a walk, so I left a note to call me at the bank as soon as possible.

Wei Lei called about fifteen minutes after I returned to my office. "Sorry, we missed you. It's such a beautiful day that I wanted them to enjoy the sunshine. We walked about two miles, and now they're taking a nap. They were both exhausted when we got home."

"Are you playing music for her?"

"I turned the radio in their room to a classical music station. She hasn't spent much time downstairs today."

"I picked out two albums when I was there. They're on the desk in my office."

"Thanks, you're always making life easier for me."

"Right now, it's the other way around."

Chapter Fourteen

Caitlin and I drove to Toronto with Aria on Saturday, and the uninterrupted time with them was good. Caitlin nursed Aria in the car while I went inside the airport to find Lysa, who was waiting for her luggage by the carousel.

Caitlin was walking around the car with Aria when we approached, and her eyes widened as she looked at Lysa in her slim-fitting dress and high-heeled shoes. I could tell she was shocked by Lysa's beauty, and I worried she might resent my bringing Lysa into our home while she was staying with her mother.

"Caitlin, I'm sorry to meet you under these circumstances. Aria is lovely, just like her mother," Lysa said.

"I'm a frumpy nursing mother, and you're elegant and beautiful. We do appreciate your coming to help with Lijuan."

"You look great to me. I wish I had a baby to nurse and a husband who loved me like I know Winson loves you. I'll dress more casually around the house, but from habit, I always try to put myself together when I'm in public. Winson has done plenty to help my family and me. I've never met anyone like him. I hope I can help Lijuan; it's the least I can do. You're making more of a sacrifice than I am."

"It's a big sacrifice, not living with my husband or in my home. I'm praying it won't be much longer."

We stopped for lunch at a restaurant on the drive home. The waitress made a big fuss over Aria, which delighted Caitlin and me.

During our conversation, Caitlin told Lysa, "I hope you'll be able to communicate with Lijuan, and she can relate to your experiences."

"I rarely talk about my past because it's difficult being a victim of human trafficking, especially the prostitution part. I've gone through many struggles and three abortions, which I didn't want. But the pain remains from losing a child. Even the unborn are still our children."

Aria was asleep in Caitlin's arms when I pulled into Maureen's driveway. I helped them out of the car and walked them into the house.

When she put Aria in the playpen, I said, "I don't want to go home without you and Aria."

"And I want to be in my own home with my husband. And now, there's a beautiful woman in our house who has never met anyone like you."

"She doesn't hold a candle to you. You know I only have eyes for you, my love."

She closed her eyes briefly, then rubbed her nose as she said, "You better go. It's been a long day already." I put my arms around her, kissed her, and walked to the car.

It felt strange taking Lysa inside our house with her luggage. This situation had to change quickly, even if I had to find other living arrangements for Lijuan. The kitchen was quiet, and I took Lysa upstairs to get her settled and gave her the bedroom next to the suite.

"Please make yourself at home. The closet and dresser are empty, and the bathroom has fresh towels. I'm going to check on Mother and Lijuan. I'll see you downstairs when you're ready."

Lysa thanked me, and I knocked on Mother's door, then quietly opened it when I heard her singing a lullaby.

"Look who is home, Lijuan." Mother greeted me. Lijuan sat beside her on the sofa, holding YeYe's medallion.

"How was your day?" I asked with a smile and hoped it didn't look as forced as it felt.

"We walked to the lake this morning. Lijuan is gaining strength daily, aren't you, my dearest?" Mother asked Lijuan, but she didn't respond.

"Did Wei Lei go home?" I asked.

"I sent her home after lunch. Lijuan and I are okay alone."

"Lysa is here, and I'd like you to meet her. Shall I make tea downstairs, or would you rather meet up here?"

"We'll come downstairs to the kitchen. Give us a few minutes to freshen up."

"Take your time. Lysa is unpacking. I'll see you both in the kitchen."

When I entered the kitchen, I put on the kettle and called Caitlin at her mother's. "I miss you, love. Thank you for driving with me to Toronto."

"I miss you too. Did Lysa meet Lijuan?"

"Not yet. She's unpacking. Pray all goes well. I need you and Aria home with me."

"One day at a time."

I was hanging up when Lysa walked in wearing black slacks and a green sweater. She looked lovely, and I was reminded of Caitlin's concern and turned away quickly. Lysa helped me set the table for tea, and I found cookies Rhoda had baked.

Mother walked in, guiding Lijuan in front of her. Lijuan sat at the table, and I introduced Lysa to her and Lily. Mother was cordial, but Lijuan looked Lysa up and down and said nothing.

I had told Lysa about the medallion, so she asked Lijuan about it. When Lijuan didn't respond, she asked her about YeYe and said she was fortunate to know her grandfather. Lijuan still said nothing. Then she told Lijuan she was blessed to have her mother and brother with her.

I wanted so much for her to respond, but after a few silent moments, I said, "Lijuan, I've missed you over the years. We have so many wonderful memories together growing up in Hangzhou. I'm glad you're here."

"Lysa, when did you come from China?" Mother asked.

"When I was twelve. My father was already in Canada, but we didn't know all the circumstances. The men who brought us took me away from my mother and forced me to have sex with men I did not know. The first time was harrowing, and I cried and bled for days afterward. Until that time, I never had a monthly cycle."

"My goodness, you were so young. My sweet Lijuan was only twelve years old when the Red Guard arrested me and sent me to the mountains, never to return. I was not able to say goodbye to my family. My husband was already in prison, and Wen Shun had been sent to Canada. I did not know what happened to Lijuan or my father."

"Lijuan, do you remember when I did not come home from school because I was arrested?" Mother asked.

Still, she didn't respond, but her hands trembled as she lifted the tea to her lips.

"Were you raped and forced to have sex with older men in China?" Lysa asked.

She nodded.

"Many men, or just one?" Lysa asked.

"General Bao."

"The first time I was forced to have sex, I hoped it would never happen again. There were many men, and they were awfully rough. I had several babies, but they were taken from me before birth. Did you leave babies behind?"

Tears flooded her face, but she didn't scream. If Lijuan was a concubine and not a wife, would she be allowed to have children? Maybe Lijuan was forced to abort any babies she might have conceived. My heart wept for my sister.

I called Caitlin before bed and told her about the rest of the day and the conversation. We both had difficulty imagining the horrors Lysa and Lijuan lived through as children.

☙

On Sunday morning, Lysa asked me if she could spend time alone with Lijuan because she thought Lijuan might be more willing to open up if they were alone. It was worth a try, so she took Lijuan outside by the blue spruce to enjoy the sunshine.

To settle Mother's nerves, she and I cleaned the kitchen while they were outside.

"Lijuan is getting stronger even though she is not talking. I miss Aria and Caitlin, and I know you do too. Should you bring them home?"

"This is extremely difficult for me. I miss them but need to help Lijuan. I'd like to update Bitsy on what's happening and get her advice."

"Of course. I'll finish cleaning while you call Bitsy."

Bitsy was encouraging but reminded me there was no quick fix. She was glad Lysa was there and thought it was a good idea for Lysa and Lijuan to spend private time together. She also thought it was premature to bring Aria back into the house. Lijuan had enough demons to face in her talks with Lysa without adding a baby to the equation. I didn't want to hear this but I understood Bitsy's reasoning. When I returned to the kitchen, Mother was watching Lysa and Lijuan through the window.

"They have been out there for over an hour, but I do not think Lijuan is talking," Mother said.

"Let's give them all the time they need. Maybe they'll want to walk with us when they come inside."

They returned to the house holding hands, and their eyes were bloodshot. Lijuan let go of Lysa's hand and headed for the stairs, and Mother followed right behind her.

"Lysa, I'm sorry I shouldn't have imposed on you."

A minute of uncomfortable silence went by.

"It was a good thing."

"How so?"

"I told her more about my journey and how I was abused. Certain situations I can't speak about without crying. She was silent, but when I cried, she held my hand. She wants to talk but doesn't have enough courage yet."

When she put her hand to her lips to stop the quivering, I took her in my arms until she calmed. I didn't know what to say and hoped my embrace offered comfort. However, if I'd considered my reaction beforehand, it would have been better to comfort her with words because I didn't want to give Lysa the wrong impression.

When I let go and stepped away, Lysa said, "Your sister has been through a lot, but I hope she'll come around. We need to have faith."

I endured horrible conditions on the ship and at the logging camp, but their situations were worse and lasted longer. But pain is relative to each person's threshold.

∾

Sunday evening, before she went upstairs for the night, I gave Lijuan a copy of *I Ching*, the Book of Changes. She moved her fingers over the cover, opened it, flipped through a few pages, and looked at me for the first time with acknowledgment.

"Remember when you visited Cousin Liu Yang, and her friend read your fortune with stones, and you also asked for my fortune?" She looked confused. "You told me about *I Ching*. Then, a few years ago, I was in a bookstore and found this book. It reminded me of you and being together in Hangzhou."

She frowned momentarily and looked like she had a headache, then her face relaxed.

"*I Ching* was what our cousin said had been used by emperors for over a thousand years. Do you remember the six divination coins, five the same and one different?" She was paying close attention to my words, so I continued. "You tossed them on a table, and the fortune teller explained the meaning of each one to make either yin or yang more or less likely to move."

Her cheeks turned pink like a rose petal, and she said, "Our hearts were one, and then you left."

A flower bloomed as Catherine said it might. I was so excited to hear her speak I threw my arms around her and held her in a firm embrace. "My lovely sister, you're returning to us."

To my surprise, she wrapped her arms around me and completed the embrace. I was sorry Mother had gone upstairs to bathe and didn't witness this exchange. Without thinking, I reached up and put my fingers through her hair.

She let me touch her, and even smiled as she said, "You liked to touch my hair when I was little."

I could hardly wait to call Caitlin and give her the good news. A few minutes later, Mother came downstairs and told Lijuan the bath was ready, and she noticed the smile on Lijuan's face and that she was holding the *I Ching* book in her hand.

We were finally seeing progress, and I was able to get a good night of sleep.

Chapter Fifteen

Peggy entered my office and said, "We're honored with a visitor this afternoon." She stepped aside, and filling the door frame was a familiar figure wearing a gentle smile on his chiseled face.

"Chief Kirkpatrick, welcome. How's everything with you?"

"Running smoothly." He knocked on the wooden desk. "How's your house guest?"

"Chukee's health is failing. We've moved him to Rhoda's home because I brought my sister to Collingwood a few days ago. It's been a difficult adjustment. Caitlin and Aria had to leave the house because my sister freaked over Aria. Clive's wife, Bitsy, is a licensed psychologist and thinks Lijuan's in traumatic shock and may have been taken away from her child or forced to have an abortion. It's chaos at home right now. Unfortunately, we can't commit her to a hospital because she only speaks and understands Mandarin. Once I settle my sister, I'll work with you and the RCMP to track Dung's crime syndicate. Yonge's already turned information over to the RCMP. I'm sorry I haven't kept you in the loop, but life's been hectic."

"I didn't come to talk about the Chinese syndicate, but I've interesting news for you." He opened a manila folder and handed me a sheet of paper. "Do you recognize the man in these photos?"

The pictures on the page were a series of black and white police mug shots. The man wore wire-rimmed glasses, his head was bald, his skin looked mottled, and his face was almost hidden by a long bushy beard and mustache.

"There's something familiar about him, but I can't put a name to the face."

"He worked with you at Merchant's Bank."

I studied the photos. "He can't be Colin Cheek!"

"I didn't recognize him either."

"He doesn't look like the man I sat beside for years."

"He was apprehended in Knife River, Minnesota, for drunk driving by a Cook County Sheriff, and we've started the paperwork for extradition. His address is in Grand Marais, Minnesota, just south of the Canadian border, on the west coast of Lake Superior. The police report said Cheek was in a fishing tournament in Knife River. Apparently, he drank more than he caught."

We both laughed.

"Is that where Cheek and Taylor crossed the border?"

"It's an open border and remote. Most anyone can cross it. Northern Minnesota is densely forested and sparsely populated with iron mines and Indian reservations. The area attracts fringe elements, so it's a good place for people to live who don't want to be found. It would have been a long drive for Taylor and Cheek but a safer place to cross the border since there was an APB out for them."

"Do you know anything more about Cheek's circumstances?"

"The Sheriff arrested him as Bob Soderberg. He was fingerprinted, and they couldn't reconcile his claimed identity with anyone registered within the State. Then, on a hunch, the sheriff checked with the RCMP, and the fingerprints matched Curtis Cheek. Because of the outstanding warrant, Cheek was transferred to the Duluth Police Department where he's being detained, pending extradition."

"Anything on Taylor?"

"Check hasn't been questioned by Canadian authorities yet, so we might consider offering him a plea bargain if he provides information on locating Taylor."

"Is there a chance to recover any of the stolen money?"

"Don't get your hopes up." He handed me an envelope with Winson written on it. "This is for you. The Duluth Police Department sent it with their file."

I didn't know what to expect but was prepared to hear more of Check's harangues. I read it aloud.

> *Winson,*
>
> *I assume you're still alive, living in Collingwood, and working for Mr. LeBlanc. I hated you from the first day I saw you in the bank.*

"Winson, stop. You can read it to yourself, but don't place any importance on what someone like Check has to say."

"I've had to put up with this ever since I left Hangzhou. It won't be anything I haven't heard before but thank you for your thoughtfulness, Chief."

> *The more Mr. LeBlanc trusted you, the more I despised you. My hatred of you was because of me. I had aspired to be like Mr. LeBlanc. I idolized him, wanted to be in his shadow, and wanted him to mentor me. My dreams ended with his accident. When Taylor was hired as the new bank manager, he threatened to fire me unless I was loyal to him. I needed the job, and I became who he wanted me to be after a while. I didn't*

like myself and started drinking too much. It set me on a course I couldn't control or pull out of, and I became callous and numb.

When you started coming into the bank with the full support and trust of Mr. LeBlanc, I hated you even more and envy ate me up. I was out of control, and what I did wasn't right, and I'm sorry.

I lost everything when Taylor and I fled across the border. I abhorred Taylor because following him cost me my life, family, and country. A few months after we arrived in the US, we got into an intense argument over splitting the money and the crimes we had committed. We cursed each other and threw punches. I walked out of the flea-bag motel we were living in and never returned.

I was desperate and found a job with the forestry service north of Grand Marais.

I hope you won't recognize me anymore, not because I have lost 40 pounds, lost my hair, and wear a bushy beard, but because I'm not the same person. Living in the forest, sleeping in a tent, I was in an oasis of dark sky nights and saw the Milky Way and Northern Lights like never before. I was awed by the night sky and saw my squalor in the stars. It seemed the earth and stars spoke to me. I got back in touch with a part of me that was dead and returned to the feelings and goals I had as a young man.

I met a man named Kalle Wuorenmaa who was trafficked from Finland and escaped from a logging operation like you had. When he shared his story with me, my conscience burdened me even more, and I couldn't escape it. I saw your face in my dreams and couldn't seem to get rid of them. I knew I needed to make amends for the way I treated you.

I know I should have turned myself in, and I'm honestly thankful I was arrested in Knife River. I want to take responsibility for my actions, pay my debt to the Province, and try to repay you for what I embezzled. I will not fight extradition and will accept my punishment. Soon, I will hear the prison door shutting, but I can give you my apology today and ask for your forgiveness.

I wish I could help you find Taylor, but I don't know where he went. It wouldn't surprise me if he left Minnesota. He obtained a Minnesota driver's license under the name of Charles Adams.

I have carried a burden over what I did to you and hope you can find mercy to forgive me. I wish you and your family the best.

Sincerely,
Colin Cheek

"I've seen criminals write letters to their mothers asking for forgiveness when they faced capital punishment, but this is the first time I've seen someone like Cheek offer restitution," Kirkpatrick said.

"Cheek's letter spoke to my heart. When he faces his charges, would you ensure this letter is presented to the Crown?"

He folded the letter, slid it back into the envelope, and said, "I'm glad I've gotten to know you, and I'll make sure to deliver this letter to the prosecutor with your remarks."

"What about Avant?"

"I received nothing from him except sneers when I saw him last week after your call."

Before Kirkpatrick left my office, Peggy rushed to the door. "Winson, Caitlin's on the phone and said it is an emergency."

"I'll leave you to your phone call," Kirkpatrick said.

"Please wait." I picked up the phone and said, "Love, what's wrong?"

"I think Chukee's dead. I left Rhoda with him and Aria by the lake, where we watched the ducks and swans. She's trying to resuscitate him."

"Where are you?"

"At a pay phone near the park."

"Chief Kirkpatrick is with me. We'll be right there." I told Kirkpatrick and he drove me to the lake with the siren on. On the way, he called dispatch to have an ambulance meet us there. When we arrived, Rhoda was still trying to revive Chukee. The ambulance pulled up a few minutes later, and the paramedics took over. Chukee's color was ashen, and when the paramedic tried to find his pulse, he shook his head and asked, "How long have you been giving him CPR?"

"I don't know, maybe fifteen minutes," Rhoda said.

"I think he's passed, but we'll transport him to the hospital just to be sure."

"We'll follow you there," Kirkpatrick replied.

Caitlin pulled me aside and said, "I need to settle my emotions and want to walk home with Aria if that's okay. Can Rhoda ride with you?"

I put my arms around her and attempted to kiss her lips, but she turned her cheek to me. "Whatever is best for you, love," I said and then turned to Aria, kissed her head, and said, "Love you, sweet girl."

Aria raised her arms for me to pick her up, but Caitlin stepped in and lifted Aria into her arms. "I'll take Aria to Mother's house and meet you at the hospital."

I hated to see them walk away. It was unlike her to turn her cheek, and also to not want me to take her home. Anyone would be unsettled from actually seeing Chukee die, but her response was something more. I felt distanced from her, probably from the upheaval at home.

Rhoda and I put the wheelchair in the trunk and got in the police car with Kirkpatrick. When we arrived at the hospital, the paramedics took Chukee inside, and Rhoda followed the gurney into the emergency room.

Kirkpatrick was kind enough to go inside with me and talk to the charge nurse.

"We'll need the man's name. Do you know what was wrong with him?" the nurse asked.

"His name is Chukee Dung."

"Does he have a doctor?"

Before I could answer, Rhoda walked up, and the expression on her face told me Chukee was gone.

I put my arms around her and said, "You did your best to bring him back. You've been a blessing to Chukee these past few months. He was happy when he was with you."

The nurse interrupted and said, "Sir, does he have a doctor?"

"He doesn't need a doctor. He passed."

"I'm glad his pain is over and I took him to the lake today. If I could have known it was his last one, I would..."

The nurse interrupted again to ask Chief Kirkpatrick about an autopsy.

"No foul play was involved. Rhoda and the paramedics made every effort to try and revive him, so there's no need for one," the Chief replied.

Rhoda returned to the cubicle to wait with Chukee's body, and Kirkpatrick returned to the police station while I made arrangements with Drott's Funeral Home.

Caitlin arrived before Drott picked up Chukee. I held her in my arms before I spoke. "This is all so overwhelming. I need you and Aria back home so we can live together as we should."

"Rhoda needs us now. She was especially fond of Chukee, and there'll be a void for her, especially since her students graduated and are moving out in a few days."

"We'll be there for her."

"Maybe we could move in with Rhoda."

"I'd rather have you and Aria at home."

Chapter Sixteen

A few weeks later, Rhoda came to the bank, entered my office, and said, "You know I have a habit of sticking my nose in your business?"

"Why would you say that? You're family. Maybe someday I'll stick my nose in your business as well."

It was good to hear her laugh, but her smile disappeared as she said, "I'm worried about you and Caitlin."

"Did Caitlin say something to you?"

"She doesn't have to. I see her every day and read her like a book. She belongs with her husband, Aria belongs with her father, and they must move back home, period!"

"I'm hoping soon. Lijuan is finally making progress. She's spoken a few times to me and more to Mother and Lysa, but always one-on-one and only a few words, not a conversation."

"Do you or Lysa or Lily talk to her about Aria?"

"I want to but don't want to upset her. I'm sure Lysa does. Why do you ask?"

"Because Lijuan's not ready to see Aria yet. I baked scones and took them to your house for breakfast this morning. Lily and Lysa were in the kitchen, but not Lijuan. We heard a scream and ran, and Lijuan was on the floor in the nursery, pounding her fists and shrieking."

I buried my head in my arms on the desk. When Rhoda put her hand on my shoulder, I lifted my head and met her gaze. She said, "Listen to me. I have empty rooms and can take Lily, Lijuan, and Lysa, so Caitlin and Aria can come home."

"You're always coming to everyone's rescue. I want Caitlin and Aria with me but don't know how Lijuan will deal with being relocated. She's getting comfortable with Mother and Lysa where she is."

"She was screaming. Screaming! She wasn't comfortable today!"

This setback left me speechless.

"Sometimes I can be pretty blunt, especially when you're thick." She slapped the desk twice and repeated, "Thick as the ice on a skating rink!"

"After Chukee passed, Caitlin joked that the three of us should move in with you."

Her eyes brightened. "You'd be more than welcome. Even though I don't allow men in my house, I'd make an exception for you like I did for Chukee."

She lifted my spirits, and I couldn't help but laugh.

"I love all three of you and hate an empty house. I need family! Why don't you ask Lily if we can try it? If it doesn't work for Lijuan, we can start over."

"Are you sure?"

"Let me tell you how it is for me. Each morning I sit alone at the kitchen table, sip tea, with two empty cups on either side of me, with two plates of untouched slices of toast next to each cup. But no one comes to join me because both my men are gone."

Rhoda was unselfish and had been a part of my life since I accepted the job as Julian's caregiver. She always gave one hundred percent of herself to whatever she did and whoever she cared about. Julian had bequeathed her a nice nest egg, and the home she had shared with her husband was paid for.

"I'll talk to Caitlin, Mother, and Bitsy and let you know. Lijuan's condition has been hard on everyone."

"It's been hardest on Caitlin and Aria, but Caitlin will never tell you that."

To make the best decision, I called Bitsy for her professional opinion. When I explained the situation, she said, "Aria should not be in the same house with Lijuan yet, but moving Lijuan and Lysa to Rhoda's is an excellent idea. Lysa has been a great help to Lijuan, and I can see an improvement in her mental condition; however, you need to set boundaries, and Aria and Caitlin must move home to protect your marriage."

When I arrived at Maureen's, she told me Caitlin and Aria were napping and we could talk on the porch for a few minutes.

"This arrangement is tough for Caitlin. They've been here almost three weeks. Aria hasn't taken to sleeping in the playpen, so Caitlin and Aria sleep in the same bed. It's not good for either of them. She's your wife and deserves better than this. Are you going to choose your sister over your wife and child?"

I was shocked by her statement and blind to the pressure Caitlin was feeling. My wife and baby needed to be home, and Lijuan needed help. Rhoda was offering me the best solution, and I prayed it would work.

"I'm sorry, Maureen."

"You don't have to say you're sorry to me. You need to apologize to Caitlin."

"That's why I'm here."

"Well, she can't talk right now, and I wouldn't come back until you can take her and Aria home. I love having them here, but it's not where they belong."

"I'll return tonight to bring them home. Thank you for your honesty."

I stopped at the bank and told Peggy I would be home the rest of the day if she needed me. I didn't know how to explain everything to Mother, Lijuan, and Lysa, but I had no choice.

Mother and Lysa were at the kitchen table when I walked in the back door, and Mother asked what I was doing home so early.

"I'm bringing Caitlin and Aria home tonight. They're unsettled and need to be in their own home."

"It's too soon," Mother said, looking at Lysa for confirmation.

"Lijuan went into the nursery this morning and started screaming again. Maybe you should reconsider," Lysa said.

"I must put my marriage first. It's been too long."

"A divided house isn't good. I'll go upstairs while you explain to Lily?"

"You can stay; you're part of our family." I put my hand on Mother's arm and said, "Rhoda offered her home to Lijuan, Lysa, and you."

"I don't understand," Mother stiffened and wrung her hands together.

"It's best if I leave the two of you alone," Lysa said.

"I'll take Mother into my office."

I led her by the hand, closed the office door, and explained the stress on Caitlin and how life in Canada differed from China, she frowned, and her expression hardened.

"No. How can you be so cruel? She is getting better and must stay here. We are your family, and you would make us leave? It has been two decades since we were separated. Then a miracle happened, and you want to undo it. No, absolutely not. This is not how to honor your family. My mother and father tolerated your father to keep our family together."

"But look at the relationship I had with father. I lived separated from him in your home. You and YeYe raised me, and you had to make a pact with Father to keep the peace. I'm trying to save my marriage."

"You are the man of the house. Your wife should be obedient." She pinched her lips together and shook her head.

"This is Canada, Mother."

"All your wife wants is to spend money on clothes and shoes."

"You're misjudging her. She's a kind and generous woman who spends money on others before herself. She was reaching out to you and expressing her love. She certainly can't communicate it fully to you with words. I know this is incredibly difficult for you to understand. Lijuan has experienced severe trauma, and I'll continue to help her, but Caitlin is my wife, and I'm responsible for loving and caring for her and Aria in the same way you cared for Lijuan and me. I hope you understand, but this is the way it has to be. You can stay here and walk to Rhoda's to visit during the day, but Lysa and Lijuan must move."

"You are not my son to act like this. I will go to Rhoda's with Lijuan. I no longer want to live with you and your wife." She stormed out of my office and went upstairs.

It was difficult speaking to my mother, and I wished she'd realize my situation. I called Rhoda to make the arrangements, and when I returned to the kitchen and told Lysa they were moving and how Mother responded, she said I was doing the right thing for my family and she would speak to Lily.

Lysa wanted to share a room with Lijuan to give them more time together, and she went upstairs to talk to Lily and pack her bags.

While Lysa and Mother were talking in Lysa's room. I sat on the sofa in the suite with Lijuan. She was listening to music and reading the *I Ching* book. "Mother, Lysa, and you will stay with Rhoda for a few days. She doesn't live far from here, and I'll see you every day."

Lijuan put down the book, folded her arms, and wouldn't look at me.

"Do you like spending time with Lysa?"

"Lysa," Lijuan said as she finally looked at me.

"Yes. I'll take all three of you to Rhoda's. She has a lovely house with a big bathtub. It's a whirlpool tub where the water swirls around you.

"I like bathtub," Lijuan replied.

I took her comment as an indication of acceptance and asked her to come downstairs to have tea with me while Mother packed.

About fifteen minutes later, Lysa and Mother came downstairs, each carrying a bag. Mother wouldn't look at me, but I took them to Rhoda's house. She was cooking dinner when we walked in the door, and the aroma was wonderful. Rhoda gave each of us a big hug, including Lijuan. Lijuan didn't return her hug, but she didn't panic either. I carried the bags, and we all walked upstairs. She put Lysa and Lijuan in the same room with twin beds. The whirlpool bath was down the hall, and I asked Rhoda to show it to Lijuan and Lysa.

"I take bath here?" Lijuan asked with a smile.

"We're going to stay here for a while. Rhoda will let you bathe tonight after dinner," Lysa said.

When Mother, Rhoda, and I returned to the kitchen, Rhoda took hold of my arm and said, "Go buy Caitlin flowers, then pick her up, take her and Aria home, and you can enjoy a second honeymoon!" She laughed, then said, "Now get out of here," as she pushed me towards the door.

"Mother, I'll see you tomorrow," I said in Mandarin, but she didn't respond.

Mother's reaction upset me, but I could hardly wait to pick up Caitlin and Aria. It'd been much too long. I stopped at the florist and bought a dozen long-stemmed yellow roses for Caitlin and a small stuffed bear for Aria.

Maureen greeted me at the door and said, "I assume the gifts aren't for me!"

"They're for your beautiful daughter and grandchild."

"Caitlin and Aria aren't here. They went for a walk to the lake, but I don't know if she'll go home with you."

"I'm going to find her."

I left the flowers with Maureen, kept the stuffed bear, and headed toward the lake, hoping to find my wife and daughter. I could hear Aria's squeals of delight before I saw them sitting on a bench.

"What are you doing here?" Caitlin asked.

"Looking for you." Aria lifted her arms for me to pick her up. I gave her the bear, lifted her from the stroller, and sat next to Caitlin with Aria on my lap.

"I'm sorry I've put Lijuan and Mother before you and Aria these last few weeks. It won't ever happen again. I want you to come home. The house is empty without you."

"The house certainly isn't empty, and there's no room for Aria and me in the house or your life right now!"

"I hope you know I have no life without you and Aria. I want you home."

We haven't been alone together since Lijuan arrived."

"Not by choice."

"It is a choice. You've chosen your mother and sister over us. I can't come home with Lijuan there."

"Rhoda offered to take Mother, Lijuan, and Lisa, and I moved them a few hours ago. So it's just the three of us now."

She folded her arms, looked at the ducks, raised her voice, and said, "I'm not ready to come home."

There were furtive glances from passersby, and I lowered my voice. "Are you having second thoughts about marrying me?"-

"Why have I been staying with my mother the last three weeks, and Lysa, Lily, and Lijuan are living in my house with you?" She wouldn't look at me. "And you never told me how beautiful Lysa is, and she admitted she's never met a man like you!"

"I'm not interested in Lysa or any other woman." I reached for her hand, but she pulled away. "Please look at me. You're the only woman I've ever loved. I've made lots of mistakes and haven't handled this situation well."

"You can't give up on your sister, but we're your family too."

"I wasn't prepared for Lijuan's condition and didn't have the mental understanding to consider the unintended consequences of bringing Chukee, my mother, and sister into our home. After you lost your father and Kathleen moved out, I burdened you with all three of them, and Lijuan's behavior is overwhelming, even for me. I understand why you're upset, and I promise to never put you in that position again."

When she didn't respond, I said, "There's no excuse for how I neglected you and Aria."

"I know you're trying, but we've lost communication. A phone call once or twice a day isn't enough, and we haven't slept in the same bed in weeks. That's not a marriage."

"I can't change what's happened. All I can do is promise to make things right for us." I bowed my head and rested it on Aria's head, and she tapped me with her bear.

"You've had dreams over the years about your family as if they were calling you. Lately, my father's been calling me, making me wonder about you and our marriage. All this is too much for me, and I don't know what to do."

She burst into tears, which made Aria cry, and when she wiped her face with a handkerchief, a man sitting on a bench near us approached and said to Caitlin, "Miss, can I help you? Is this man bothering you?" He gave me a stern look and asked her, "Do you want me to call the OPP?"

"This is none of your business," I said.

"Mister, I'm making it my business."

Caitlin rubbed her eyes, then took Aria from my arms and said, "Thank you for your concern, but we're okay."

"Are you sure?"

She nodded. He ignored me, looked at Caitlin, and said, "I'll be sitting nearby watching, so just waive if you need me. A beautiful lady like you shouldn't be harassed."

I stood up to confront him, but Caitlin grabbed my arm and said, "We're fine." He walked away but kept looking at us from a nearby bench.

I was ready to punch the guy, so I took a minute to calm my nerves and sat quietly beside Caitlin. "I never wanted you to leave. You and Aria belong in your own home. If this doesn't work for Lijuan, I'll find other help for her. I want to live with you and Aria in our home if you'll have me."

"I don't know, so much has happened. Your mother will resent me for making her move, and Lijuan will need to make more adjustments. This might be a setback for her, and it'll be my fault. I realize traditions are different in China, and I don't want to be the bad wife."

"You'll never be the bad wife, and Mother will eventually understand. It doesn't work for us to be apart. I miss seeing your face first thing in the morning and holding you in my arms through the night. We were meant to be together."

She wiped her eyes, then took my hand and said, "Our love is composed of a single soul inhabiting two bodies, and we must hold hands to keep from drifting apart." Her face brightened, and she looked at me warmly and said, "Our hearts were designed to be united."

"I want to experience the wonders of the world with you and Aria. I should've set boundaries, and if Bitsy and Lysa can't help Lijuan, I'll find a rehabilitation facility for her. We'll find a solution, not involving Lijuan living with us."

She kissed me and said, "Let's go home."

When we returned to Maureen's, Kathleen was home, and we discussed our plan.

"Caitlin, if you ever let this man go, I'll be first in line," Kathleen said.

"Kathleen, you need to find your own man. Winson, I have dinner ready if you'd like to stay," Maureen said.

"I'd like to take Caitlin out for dinner. Would you be willing to keep Aria for a few hours?"

"I'm always happy to have Aria. Go enjoy time together."

Chapter Seventeen

The following two weeks were celebratory for us. Maureen and Kathleen would help Caitlin during the day, but we had the evenings and mornings to ourselves. Together we saw how Aria was changing, crawling around the floor and pulling up to a stand. We knew she would take her first steps any day.

I checked on Lijuan and Mother daily and visited during lunch several times a week and on Sundays when Caitlin went to church. Mother had warmed to the new arrangement and would visit Caitlin and Aria occasionally but spent most of her time with Lijuan.

One Sunday morning, Mother was grinning from ear to ear when I arrived and asked me to go to the backyard and talk to Lijuan. She was under a maple tree, thumbing through a women's magazine.

"Anything interesting?" I asked.

She pointed to the layout of models wearing summer dresses. "Which one do you like?"

"The dresses or the models?" I asked with a smile.

"The hairstyles, silly. I always took pride in my hair and wore it western style like Mother."

"I can make an appointment for you to get your hair styled any way you want."

"I haven't had what I want since I was twelve years old. I'm angry one minute and sad the next. What I want is a fresh start and to forget the past."

As she looked off in the distance, I became annoyed and frustrated as I reflected on how helpless I was to do anything to protect her in China even though I inherited Julian's assets. I paused to compose my emotions and said, "I know you had a difficult life after I left China. I can't change your past, but I can promise you a better future."

Her eyes were downcast as she said, "I did not have a normal life with General Bao. I was disoriented, abused, and didn't know where I belonged. It is time for me to be strong."

My heart ached for the life she had lived. "You're strong, and we'll get through this together."

She put her hand on her heart, and said, "I am grateful I can count on you, Mother, and Lysa to help me through the ups and downs."

"That's what family and friends are for, to be there in good and bad times."

"Remember the fortune teller who said you would go on a journey you did not want to take? We both went on journeys we did not want to take, you to Canada and me to General Bao." She put her arms around me like she did when we were young.

"Life's been rough for us, but we're still young and have a good deal of living to do. Canada is a good country, and you'll have a good life here."

"Lysa has helped me realize I am a victim, like her, Mother, and you. We each lived through different circumstances, but they were all trying."

"Yet here we are together, in a free country, with open opportunities ahead of us."

"I miss my babies but must make a new life without them." She took a tissue from her pocket and wiped her eyes.

"I'm sorry you lost your babies. Would you tell me about them?"

With closed eyes and a painful expression, she said, "My first baby was a girl. I was only thirteen, and Bao took her away soon after birth. My second was a boy, and Bao was delighted and allowed me to nurse him for a year but then gave him to his first wife, who hadn't had a boy. My third was another boy, and Bao said I couldn't keep him, so I hid him for a while, but the General found him when he was six months old, took him away, and punished me."

"It must've been difficult to see Aria."

"At the time, I thought she was mine. My life has been a blur since I was taken from Bao. I do not remember how I got here. Lysa has experienced many of the same issues and has been trying to help me put the pieces together." She paused to control her emotions.

We sat in silence for a few minutes.

"Tell your wife I am sorry."

"Caitlin understands and is willing to bring Aria to see you when you're ready."

"It is too soon for me to hold a baby. It hurts too much." Then she lifted YeYe's medallion from her neck. "YeYe gave this to you. You must keep it."

"If you had been boarding the ship on that cold November day, he would have given it to you. It belongs to both of us. I wore it for eighteen years; now it's your turn."

"I am getting a new hairstyle, and Lysa is taking me shopping for clothes." She put her hand on mine. "I am starting a new life and want new things, so keep the medallion. It looks better on you anyway."

"Well, this calls for a celebration. I'm paying for the new clothes and treating all four of you ladies to a trip to the beauty shop."

⌇

Bitsy told me that our human psyche has a protective mechanism that blocks out traumatic events to allow us to survive those experiences. She referred to a disassociated process where the conscious mind closes, and the subconscious registers what's happening and stores it. But then, there can come a time when the conscious mind feels safe enough to acknowledge those things, and the memories can be recovered. With emotional trauma, the body keeps score and remembers. In Lijuan's case, her body remembered the bad things, and the good things had been locked away from her conscious mind. I didn't understand everything, but I was glad Lijuan was improving, and I could hardly wait to give Caitlin the news.

Each person's trauma and threshold for pain were unique.

Chapter Eighteen

David Yonge called a few days later and said he had meetings in Ottawa and Toronto and wanted to visit us in Collingwood for the weekend. I arranged to pick him up in Toronto on Saturday morning.

Caitlin and I planned a dinner party for Saturday night with Kai and Wei Lei preparing a traditional Chinese dinner. Rhoda offered to watch Aria in the nursery so Caitlin would be free to enjoy our guests and Aria could sleep in her own bed. Caitlin invited her mother, Kathleen, Catherine and Yves, Joseph Lawrence and his girlfriend, Julia. In addition, I asked Clive and Bitsy, Chief Kirkpatrick and his wife, Mother, Lijuan, and Lysa. Catherine called Friday and canceled because she wasn't feeling well, and Joseph and Julia were unavailable.

It was after eleven o'clock on Saturday morning when I picked up David at his Toronto hotel. He dressed in a golf shirt and casual slacks and carried a brown leather briefcase, a small suitcase, and a garment bag. We drove to Collingwood, and I gave him a tour of the harbor area and Hurontario Street, and when I pointed out Merchants Bank, he wanted to see inside, so we stopped, and I showed him around.

When we pulled into my driveway, his mouth gaped open, and he said, "Wow!"

"It's known as the wedding cake house. Julian LeBlanc built it for his wife after the bank became successful."

"The swags on the facia make it look like a wedding cake. It's magnificent."

"I've lived here so long now, I don't notice its beauty or size, but I was overwhelmed the first time I saw it. We've many guest rooms, so I hope you return often."

"You may tire of me. After three days, a house guest starts to smell like fish."

"We don't have a three-day rule, so consider it an open invitation."

We entered through the front door, and I put his luggage at the bottom of the stairs, and we heard voices coming from the kitchen.

"We've dear friends cooking a traditional Chinese dinner for you tonight. They're hoping to open a Chinese restaurant in Collingwood soon. We've invited several guests. I hope you don't mind."

"I enjoy meeting people and look forward to getting to know your family and friends."

As we entered the kitchen, David said loudly, "Smells wonderful here. Reminds me of home."

Heads turned, and when the women saw this tall, handsome man, they straightened their aprons and adjusted their hair. Everyone spoke at once with a polyglot of languages.

David held up his hands and said in English and I translated, "My Mandarin is rusty, and I don't want to distract the cooks, so let's talk at dinner."

Mother bowed before him and thanked him for all he did for us in Vancouver and for processing the citizenship applications. Caitlin also thanked him and welcomed him to our home. Kathleen seemed embarrassed, maybe because of the food stains on her apron or her curly brown hair falling out of a bun, but she giggled and gushed over him.

"If you ladies and Kai will excuse us, I'll show David to his room and let him get settled."

As we went upstairs, I said, "You made quite an impression in the kitchen. There'll be several attractive ladies at dinner tonight who might start fighting over you."

"I've never had women fight over me before, but I'll look forward to it."

"Take your time freshening up. We'll have drinks in my office when you're ready."

When David came downstairs, I asked Kai to join us in my office and poured Macallan single malt scotch for us. When I served Kai, he said, "Thanks, Doc, but I don't drink on the job. I'm training to run a top-notch restaurant." I was surprised but decided not to comment. This was a major change for Kai.

"Tell me about this restaurant you're starting." David said.

"Our plans are preliminary, we're working on recipes, which you'll be served tonight. We're expecting our first child in a few months, so we'll probably wait to open the restaurant until the baby is born and Wei Lei's parents come to help."

"It's good to have family close. Chinese restaurants are usually family operations and can be remarkably successful. I took Winson to one of my favorites in Ottawa."

"You can critique our food and presentation after dinner. They're traditional Chinese dishes with a few tweaks. I hope you like spicy food."

"I'm Chinese, of course I like spicy food. My favorite dish is eggplant with garlic sauce."

"Well, you're in luck, it's one of the dishes tonight. I should return to the kitchen and help Wei Lei, it takes hours of preparation to fix this much food, and we appreciate the opportunity your visit has given us to test our recipes."

" I noticed you called Winson, 'Doc.' Why?"

"On our voyage to Canada, a cyclone in the Atlantic battered the ship, and all of the boys from China and Korea were sick except Winson. He worked in the kitchen, made Lily's tea concoction with lemongrass, and gave it to us. One boy was so sick he couldn't drink the tea, so Winson sat up and nursed him all night. By morning he could sit up. Many of those boys thought they would die, and when the storm worsened, they hoped they would. I was one of them."

After Kai returned to the kitchen, David said, "The citizenship papers for Lily are in process, and she should be a citizen of Canada within a year. Will Lijuan be able to sign her paperwork while I'm here?"

"She'll be here for dinner tonight and can execute them. You won't recognize her. Lysa Wu, who is also coming for dinner, has done an amazing job bringing Lijuan out of the trauma she experienced."

"Is Lysa a psychologist?"

"No, she's a sex trafficking victim who speaks English and Mandarin. My attorney's wife, Bitsy, is a psychologist, and she's coaching Lysa. I'm indebted to them."

"I'd like to hear Lysa's story."

"She's the one to tell you."

Caitlin came into the office with Aria on her hip. "I'd like to introduce you to the youngest LeBlanc. This is our daughter, Catherine Aria, but we call her Aria." When David smiled at her, she buried her head against Caitlin, then peaked at David when he wasn't looking.

"What a charming name for a beautiful girl. She must be a good sleeper to withstand all the chatter in this house."

"She likes her naps, and she's been growing like a weed, so sleeping must help."

"Is there anything I can help with in the dinner preparations?" I asked.

"You can entertain Aria for a while. Kathleen went home to clean up, and I must do the same. Lily is still helping Kai and Wei Lei. Dinner is set for seven, cocktails at six o'clock when the rest of our guests should arrive."

"Close the door, and I'll let her crawl around the floor. Maybe she'll take her first steps."

"If she does, you'd better call me." Neither of us wanted to miss any firsts with our daughter.

Rhoda and Maureen arrived at five-thirty while Caitlin was nursing Aria. Rhoda suggested they take Aria to Maureen's and bring her back at about ten o'clock. Caitlin would have none of it and insisted on putting Aria to bed before dinner so Rhoda and Maureen could join the party. Rhoda insisted she wasn't dressed for dinner, but I encouraged them to stay, which they did.

Kathleen arrived about fifteen minutes later. Her hair was styled, and she wore a beautiful green dress that complimented her figure. She had a radiant smile, and I could tell she was trying to impress David, who was complimentary and told her how beautiful she looked. Her smile reached all the way to her eyes.

Clive, Bitsy, Chief Kirkpatrick, and his wife, Donna, arrived next. Rhoda was quick to step up and offer drinks.

Minutes later, the front door opened, and as Lijuan and Lysa entered, my jaw dropped when I saw them, and everyone turned to look when they heard 'oohs' and 'aahs.' They were knock-out gorgeous and wore simple but elegant dresses. They had spent the afternoon getting new hairstyles, and Lijuan wore makeup for the first time in my memory.

Mother had been helping in the kitchen, and had showered and changed upstairs. I could see the pride in her eyes when she saw Lijuan, who appeared overwhelmed by the gazes. Lysa took hold of her hand and whispered something in her ear. I stepped up to make introductions, taking them each on an arm.

"David, you remember my sister, Lijuan?"

"Indeed I do," he said with a slight bow. "A pleasure to see you again, Lijuan," he said in broken Mandarin.

She returned his bow, lowered her eyes to the floor, and whispered in Mandarin, "Thank you for all you did for me."

"And this is our good friend, Lysa Wu, whose kindness to our family has been a God send. Lysa, please meet David Yonge. He's a friend from Vancouver and a Parliament Member."

He bowed, then extended his hand, saying, "Miss Wu, any friend of Winson's is a friend of mine. I'm delighted to meet you."

She tilted her head, reached out, tentatively took his hand, and said, "It's an honor, Mr. Yonge."

"Please call me David." As he spoke to her, she smiled, and his eyes sparkled.

Rhoda kept everyone's cocktails replenished, and Mother hovered over Lijuan until it was time to eat dinner.

Kai and Wei Lei insisted on serving everyone but eventually sat to enjoy the meal with us. I translated all the conversations during dinner so no one was left out.

David told us his mother and father migrated from Guangdong Province, but both had passed. He was born in Victoria in 1924, eight months after the implementation of the second Chinese Immigration Exclusion Act. His father registered his birth with the Canadian authorities and was given a certificate proving he was born in the Province, and at the bottom of the certificate were the words, 'This certificate conveys no legal status on the above.' Imagine how he felt when he discovered he was born in Canada but was deemed a non-person in the eyes of the Canadian government, couldn't own land in many neighborhoods, and was barred from practicing pharmacy, medicine, or law.

Many of us understood what it felt like to be a non-person. Whenever you mentioned the word Chinaman to a Canadian, he would conjure up visions of a cook, houseboy, waiter, farmer, laundry man, but never a doctor, accountant, or lawyer.

"From what I've read, you were instrumental in obtaining citizenship rights for Chinese in Canada and were the first to be elected to represent them in Parliament. Tell us how that came about," Clive said.

"Clive, you know better than to ask a politician an open ended question or hand him a microphone in front of an audience. There are many other topics we can discuss tonight."

"It's not often we get to spend an evening with a PM in Collingwood. We want to hear your story," Kathleen said, and the others chimed in with similar appeals.

He pushed back in his chair, looked around the table at each of us, then spoke in intervals, giving me time to translate. "During WWII, politicians were wary of calling up Chinese residents because military service would give them justification for the franchise, which meant citizenship and all the rights of being Canadian. Prime Minister Mackenzie King was one of the biggest opponents. We weren't Canadian citizens, but we were British subjects. By 1944, the Japanese Army had moved into Southeast Asia, and Britain was desperate to regain control of its Southeast Asian colonies. Winston Churchill wired King with instructions to recruit Chinese to infiltrate British owned Southeast Asia territories and organize guerrilla warfare against the Japanese. Every Chinese man of military age in BC was conscripted, and over six hundred of us were called out. At Chinese town hall meetings, elders questioned why we should fight for a country that denied us citizenship, but others said, this was our chance, and when we returned home, we could demand a franchise. There was a deliberate decision to fight overseas, specifically to obtain full citizenship.

"We were young, adventurous, with our buddies going overseas, and we didn't think about dying. Several of you met Joe, Ross, and Benny in Vancouver. We joined the Army and underwent commando training for covert missions and jungle warfare. It was thought that Chinese Canadians would blend in and be able to speak local languages. We parachuted behind enemy lines in Borneo, conducted espionage, and trained local resistance movements to sabotage Japanese supply lines and equipment. We were told if captured by the Japanese, our government wouldn't rescue us, and we'd be treated as spies, tortured, and killed. We were given cyanide pills, and there were no rules of war or the Geneva Convention for us. We took an oath of secrecy for twenty-five years, so I've never discussed our activities except to commanding officers.

"Our men experienced disease, injury, and death. I held several in my arms as they took their last breath. What we saw and experienced as a group bound us together for life and was no different from what other squads experienced in the European and Pacific theaters. When I returned home, I was determined to fight for our citizenship because these men deserved to be rewarded for their sacrifice to our country."

After listening to his story, everyone stared at him with admiration for what he'd experienced until Kathleen said, "You took a great risk, and it was at a great cost."

"After the war, there was no guarantee the Canadian government would recognize our contribution or give us full rights of Canadian citizenship. We took a gamble like many of you did when you left home to come to Canada."

"You advocated for those who had been overlooked," Lysa said.

"One of my goals in life is to represent those without a voice."

"We appreciate your sacrifice fighting for Canada. I'm sorry the government hasn't always treated Chinese and other people of color kindly. What happened when you returned?" Clive asked.

"It was 1946, and I took advantage of veterans' benefits to complete a Bachelor of Arts and a law degree at the University of British Columbia. The next year, the provincial government ended restrictions on voting for Chinese Canadians, the federal government revoked its discriminatory immigration law, and I became a full citizen. But few firms wanted to hire a Chinese lawyer, so I began a sole practice as a lawyer after graduating in 1953."

"How did you become involved in politics?" Donna Kirkpatrick asked.

"When you see others risk their lives for our children's future, it makes a deep impression. I campaigned to redress wrongs committed against our people who were born here or immigrated. I ran for office in a provincial election in 1956 and finished second, which was a moral victory."

"Why was losing a moral victory?" Bitsy asked.

"My candidacy was the first by a Chinese Canadian for a seat in any Canadian legislature, and it would've been a miracle to win. A year and a half later, I won the election and became the first Chinese Parliament Member, which newspapers termed a shocking upset."

"Why was it so shocking? You're obviously intelligent, educated, and extraordinarily handsome," Kathleen said. Caitlin glanced at me, and we were astounded by her uncharacteristic boldness.

"Thank you for the compliment. I ran against a veteran of the First World War, who was defense minister in the Liberal government, and here I was, a 33-year-old upstart in a district of about 1,400 Chinese Canadian residents."

"Wow, that's incredible," Kathleen said with elbows on the table, hands under her chin, and a big grin as she gazed at David.

"Can you tell us a little about your time in office?" Lysa asked.

"There were difficult times and people along the way, but I've earned respect among my colleagues. I've focused on having our government grant amnesty to those Chinese who came to Canada under false names. A few years ago, I was sent to the United Nations to represent the Legal Committee from Canada. In New York, I took my seat, and an usher came over and said, 'I'm sorry, sir, but this seat is reserved for the Canadian delegation,' and I replied, 'I am the Canadian delegation.'"

Laughter erupted, and when everyone settled, he said, "I don't think anyone could understand the surge of emotions I experienced from this opportunity. To go from the status of a non-person and rise to the position of representing Canada before the United Nations in a few years. It was definitely a wow moment."

"Many of us here tonight owe you our thanks," Lysa said.

"And I hope our people can become a new generation in Canada who can make significant contributions to the community in the professions, business, art, education, and banking, like our host." He pointed at each of us from China and said, "You have the blood of 5,000 years of Chinese culture running through your veins, but that doesn't stop you from loving Canada and giving your allegiance and loyalty to her."

Clive lifted his glass and toasted by saying, "I salute the progress of the Canadian government through the efforts of David and his fellow MP's to make life better for Chinese immigrants."

"We're not quite through toasting." Caitlin raised her glass and said, "Lily and Lijuan, I'm glad you're here in our home, and we can be a family. Winson and I have prayed for many years for you to be reunited." Caitlin looked directly at Mother and Lijuan as she spoke, and they both smiled at Caitlin and bowed their heads toward her. I hoped I translated with the proper emotion as we all clanked glasses.

The conversation at dinner was a mix of languages, but everyone enjoyed themselves. Before the guests departed, David said, "Tonight was special for me, not only for the wonderful food reminding me of mother and the meals we enjoyed at home but for the interactions amongst everyone."

He kissed the hand of each of the ladies and shook hands with the men.

Clive and Bitsy were the last to leave, and Clive said, "I read about you in the papers, but I had no knowledge of your history or the circumstances behind your accomplishments. So I appreciate what you shared with us tonight."

Kai and Wei Lei headed to the kitchen to clean up, but David stopped them and said, "I was impressed with your food tonight. Winson said there are no good Chinese restaurants in Collingwood. Have you picked a name?"

"Wei Lei's Café," Kai said with a big grin on his face.

"My husband is too kind. We haven't made a decision on the name. He'll be doing most of the work at first because of the baby." Wei Lei's smile was contagious.

"Whatever you name it, I'd be delighted to invest as a silent partner, and it would provide an excuse to return frequently to Collingwood."

Wei Lei's eyes opened wide, and Kai's eyebrows raised while his jaw dropped open. When he regained his composure, Kai expressed his sincere appreciation to David and said they would be in contact.

⌒

The following day, when I asked Caitlin to take Aria to church so David and I could go to Rhoda's house for Lijuan to sign her immigration papers, she said, "Mum will be delighted to show her off, but you better call Rhoda's and give them fair warning."

"Why?"

"My naïve husband. There was a buzz among the women over David's dashing good looks and elegant manner. Lysa and Lijuan are going to want to look their best for him. Last night Kathleen told me she and Mum would pick me up this morning. You know Kathleen was smitten and wants to see David again. She'll be looking picture-perfect when she gets here. Wait and see! I haven't seen her gush over a man since high school."

I called Rhoda and said we'd be there about half past ten. She said we'd better make it eleven because they were still asleep and would need time to dress.

I fixed tea and oatmeal for breakfast and was feeding Aria when David entered the kitchen and said, "The dinner party last night was wonderful, but I felt like I monopolized the conversation."

"Nonsense. Everyone wanted to hear your story and get to know you."

"Tell Kai and Wei Lei I'm serious about being a partner in their restaurant. The food they prepared was wonderful, especially the eggplant, but I overate."

"That's why we've oatmeal and fruit this morning."

"One of my favorite breakfasts, next to congee. As a bachelor, I don't do much cooking."

"You'll be getting leftovers for lunch."

"I'd like to take you and Caitlin, Lily, Lijuan, and Lysa out for dinner tonight."

"We haven't taken Lily and Lijuan to a restaurant yet."

"It's about time, don't you think?"

Kathleen and Maureen walked in the back door carrying a box smelling of cinnamon. Caitlin was right, Kathleen wore a new dress, and her hair and makeup were model perfect. She usually went first to Aria and hugged her, but this day she kissed Aria on the top of her head and headed directly toward David.

"We baked an apple cinnamon coffee cake for breakfast. We didn't think you'd be cooking after last night's meal." Kathleen set the box on the table and removed the contents releasing a wonderful aroma into the room as Caitlin walked into the kitchen.

"Winson, what did you cook that smells so good?" Caitlin asked.

"Not me," I pointed at Kathleen.

"Hi, Kathy, Mum. What are you doing here so early?

"We decided to bring breakfast to you," Kathleen said, grinning from ear to ear.

"What a pleasant surprise. Which of you will get Aria ready for church while I enjoy my favorite coffee cake and tea?"

Maureen took Aria in her arms, kissed her, and said, "I'll do it. This will be the first time we've taken her to church, and my friends will be delighted to see her."

I watched Kathleen fuss over David, and he enjoyed her attention. Caitlin looked at me with an 'I told you so' smile.

When the ladies left for church, I said to David, "I forgot to have Lijuan sign her papers last night. The ladies won't be ready for visitors until eleven, so we've time to kill. It's a perfect morning for a walk, and we've wonderful nature trails, or we can walk to the lake. Are you game?"

"I didn't bring any casual clothes."

"The temperature is warm enough for shorts and a light shirt. We're about the same size. I'll give you something to wear."

We walked for over an hour and had an interesting conversation. When we reached the waterfront, David pointed to the Nottawasaga Lighthouse on an island in the bay and said, "A lighthouse provides safe passage for ships around treacherous shoals and shallow waters. You and I are two men born oceans apart, but we can work together to change the future of immigrants in this country. You have strength of character, integrity, and a commitment to justice, which are a leader's touchstones. I'd like you to consider running for Parliament."

"I'm honored you'd consider me, but I currently have enough drama in my life. I'll keep an open mind and talk to Caitlin when our lives settle down."

When he asked about Lijuan, I shared our difficulties with her and the blessing Lysa had been. We also discussed the syndicate, Eng, D'Arcy Island, and I expressed my hope the RCMP would be able to shut down the syndicate and that my exposure to them would end.

When our walk was over, we showered and drove to Rhoda's. Lysa answered the door with a bright smile and had tea and scones on the dining table. We accepted the tea but declined the scones and explained we had eaten several pieces of Kathleen's apple cinnamon coffee cake.

"Where's Lijuan?" I asked.

"She's on the back porch enjoying the sunshine."

"Excuse me while I talk to her for a few minutes."

"I'll enjoy Lysa's company, so take your time." David looked at her with a gleam in his eyes.

"You're very kind..." Lysa was saying as I walked out the back door.

"How's my beautiful sister? I like your new clothes and hairdo." Her shiny black hair was shoulder length with a slight flip at the bottom. "Did you enjoy shopping with Lysa?"

"She is good for me. I have never had a friend like her."

"Are you content living here?"

"Oh, yes. Rhoda is kind and direct." She paused briefly, and then turned away and looked at me though her lowered eyes. "And I enjoy her bathtub."

"David's in the house and has immigration papers for you to sign. Your papers say Lijuan Tao, and Mother's say Lily Tao because, in Canada, we put the family name last."

"Mother said you and David would be coming. I will sign them, but I can only write in Mandarin."

When we went inside, Mother was in the dining room with David and Lysa. We joined them, and David said, "Lily, I lost my mother twenty years ago, but I see her spirit in you. Winson said you graduated from university. What a rare accomplishment for a woman in China."

"My father made it possible. He had a university degree and believed in the value of education, so I was sorry Winson's education was circumvented by Mao's takeover. The plan was for him to continue his education while living with a Chinese family in Canada."

"Your son's intelligence and experience go far beyond what he would have gained through a college degree program."

Chapter Nineteen

I drove David back to Toronto Monday morning and was at the bank by nine o'clock. On my desk was a letter from Eng informing me the syndicate boss wanted to meet me. Anita said the letter had arrived by courier. The fact it was hand delivered concerned me because it meant the syndicate had men in Collingwood. I hoped receiving Mother and Lijuan would be my last encounter with Eng and the crime ring, but the thought was self-deception.

I called Chief Kirkpatrick, and when I told him about Eng's letter, he asked, "Do you know the man's name?"

"Eng didn't tell me, but he did say he was from the Dawson Creek area."

"I've heard mention of a crime boss named Tai Huen. There are warrants out for his arrest across the provinces. The RCMP reports indicated he's a particularly nasty fellow. We'll alert the authorities in Dawson Creek and Vancouver. If he's here, let's hope we find him."

I was reluctant to get Eng in trouble because he allowed Kai and me to escape and brought Mother and Lijuan to me, albeit at Dung's request.

The Chief broke my thoughts as he said, "Winson?"

"Sorry, I was preoccupied with old memories. Do you want me to bring the letter and envelope to the station for prints?"

"As soon as possible."

&

Early Sunday morning, I fed Aria, then left for Rhoda's to spend time with Mother, Lijuan, and Lysa. Rhoda came out the front door as I approached, hugged me, and said, "Have fun. I'm going to meet Caitlin and take your sweet baby to church."

No one was in the kitchen or family room, so I went out on the back porch, and Mother and Lijuan were enjoying morning tea.

"Purple clay cup," Lijuan said in English as she lifted her purple cup.

"Very good, Lijuan. I remember YeYe had his tea in a purple clay cup."

She looked confused, so I repeated my words in Mandarin, and in broken English, she said, "Try learn English, Lysa teaching." Then, in Mandarin, she said, "My memories from childhood are returning."

"Hold on to the good ones."

"You are in all the good ones."

"Where's Lysa?"

"Upstairs, talking to David on the phone," Mother said.

"David Yonge?" I asked.

"Do I know another David in Canada?" Mother smirked. "He has been calling every day to talk to her. You know Lysa is beautiful."

"But not as beautiful as Caitlin or Lijuan."

"You are too kind, my brother."

"Wei Lei said they found a possible restaurant location, and Kai wants to show it to you this week. Wei Lei was nervous because the baby is due in six weeks, so I told her Lijuan and I would help Kai with the restaurant. It will give us both something to do," Mother said.

I stopped to see Kai on my way home and asked about their restaurant plans.

"We're working on pricing and menus. Wei Lei's parents are coming this week."

"You've received much support for this project which is impressive. Have you heard from David?"

"He's coming back in a few weeks to see our menus and review our budget."

"I can help you with the budget, and we can write a business plan and loan request to be submitted for approval by the finance committee."

"You would do that for us?"

"Collingwood needs a good Chinese restaurant, and Wei Lei and you will be good operators. Let's drive around town and look at locations."

We drove around and found three possible sites. Kai wrote down the phone numbers as I drove.

"Tomorrow, call for rent prices and lease terms," I said.

"Would you make the first call so I can listen and learn how to handle the questions, and then I can make calls on the other buildings?"

"In the past, you'd have wanted me to make all the calls. It's nice to see the change in your thought process."

"I have a wife and baby on the way and need to prepare, but I don't have a huge amount of confidence. I saw you change; how did you do it?"

"Not by myself. I needed change agents to help me. Someone who experienced disappointments, survived and grew from it, and who can be an example for you. As soon as I met Catherine and Julian, I started my transformation. They were my agents, my mentors. Change comes step by step, not all at once, and you grow through challenges and solving problems."

"On the ship to Canada, you told me to look forward, not behind, and learn the language and customs. The Hangzhou boys and I made fun of you for that. You were different from us."

"YeYe taught me about setting goals for myself, asking questions, and looking beyond the surface for what is happening with people because so many things aren't as they appear. For example, look at how our friendship with Joseph Lawrence has grown."

"He was the only person in Collingwood who looked beyond the color of our skin and rented us a room." Kai lowered his head and thought for a moment. "I wish Wei Lei and I had never gone to Timmins. It was a horrible experience between working in the mines and her sexual assault by the restaurant owner."

"You can recover from anything if you decide you want to. Lysa had to sleep with Dung, Tak, and many other men to save her family, and now she's making a better life for herself. Julian was paralyzed from the neck down, and Catherine is blind, and look what they overcame. We witnessed their courage each day. The best attribute for adjusting to Canadian culture is to be the best we can be at whatever task we're given."

"To build a future for my family, I need mentors like David Yonge and you."

"We're both here for you."

❧

Caitlin was in the kitchen and I said, "Lijuan said a few English words and remembered more of our childhood. Bitsy said her memories were still there and could be unlocked."

"Is Lijuan ready to see Aria?"

"She said it's still too soon. She wants to hold her but feels it'll be too painful to give her back. Maybe when Wei Lei's baby is born, it'll help Lijuan."

"Speaking of Wei Lei, she and Kai seem excited about this restaurant idea. They deserve a chance at success."

I kissed her neck and rubbed her thigh. "I see a smile on your face. Could I interest you in a little hanky-panky?"

"Did I ever tell you, you have a way with words, my love?"

Chapter Twenty

A few weeks later, Mother wanted to spend time with Aria while Caitlin and Rhoda attended church. Mother and I had tea in the kitchen while Aria played in her cupboard. "What does chink mean?" Mother asked.

I was surprised and asked, "Where did you hear that? Did someone call you a chink?"

"Kai talked about being called a chink."

"It's an offensive term for someone from China."

"Will Aria be called a chink?"

"If I'm around and someone calls her that, I'll get in their face really quick, but in the long run I can't protect her from what others will say. We'll teach her to be proud of her heritage, the importance of character, and to listen to her inner voice, just like you taught me."

Aria banged a pot and lid together, then threw them toward us. Mother laughed and said, "She's restless. Can we take her for a walk?"

"You change her while I clean the kitchen, then we'll walk to the lake."

"I like being a grandmother, even if you give me the stinky jobs," she chuckled.

When Mother returned to the kitchen with Aria, she asked, "Who owns the fancy black car in front of the house?"

"I don't know. I'll check while you put Aria in her stroller but stay in the kitchen."

I looked out the front porch window and saw two Chinese men get out of a four-door black Cadillac Fleetwood with dark-tinted windows. When the doorbell rang, I opened the door and tried to step outside, but a large man with a barrel chest and massive arms blocked the doorway. There was a bulge under his dark leather jacket.

When he moved aside, a smaller man twirling the rings on his fingers looked at me and said, "Hello, shoemaker, aren't you going to invite us in?" He was slender and dressed in a business suit with slicked-back black hair tied in a small ponytail. Peggy had said a Chinese man with a ponytail came into the bank and asked for me when I was in Vancouver.

The hulk scanned the room behind me, but I stood my ground, and my body tensed, expecting a fight. I was prepared to give my life to protect Aria and Mother.

"I wanted to meet the person all the talk has been about." He looked me over with a penetrating stare.

"And you are?" I asked.

"Tai Huen." The musk smell of his cologne was overpowering, and either he had lost his sense of smell or was ignorant and trying to impress people with how much money he could spend. He wore a plastic smile on his face as if trying to ingratiate himself and continued playing with his rings. "I'd like to meet your pretty white wife," he said.

"We can talk on the porch." I was trembling inside and didn't know what to expect.

When he motioned for his bodyguard to move, I stepped forward and closed the door behind me, wishing I could lock it.

"I understand our bank is doing well, and you've been busier than a cat covering up ten pounds of shit. I'm glad you're growing our capital," Huen said.

"I don't have your capital." The bodyguard moved behind me, and chills went up my back. I needed to stay between these two men and the front door. I was outnumbered, and in fear for my family's safety.

"You remember when Dung delivered $100,000 to you for a partnership interest in Merchant's Bank!"

"I never saw the money before it was confiscated by the OPP. If you want to collect it, you can contact the OPP or the RCMP, and I can put you in touch with either agency."

"I don't deal with the law. I have my own justice system, and you will pay!"

I needed to show firmness, and yet, not push him to an extreme. "I also have a letter from Dung stating the $100,000 belonged to me with no strings attached."

He rocked back and forth from one foot to the other and said, "Dung's letter means nothing to me. Ours is an arrangement like buying insurance, offering protection for you, your family, Merchant's Bank, and Kai and Wei Lei. Oh, and let me not forget to include Lysa Wu and her parents in the coverage." He was astute, articulate, and threatening as he stared at me momentarily, then said, "From time to time, I'll call on you for a favor like one would from a country club friend."

"There'll be no protection payments from me. You leave my family alone, and I won't say anything to the authorities about your operations."

His face hardened. "Are you bloody kidding me? We're already partners, and you have benefited from our relationship."

"I would lose the bank if any partners were wanted by the RCMP."

"You're already excluded from banking social circles. Other bankers want you to know your place and will eventually force you out of the business. You will benefit from our political connections, and we have ways to work around the law."

He delighted in making me uncomfortable, but I wouldn't cross a line. "I have a good reputation in the banking industry and have colleagues in high places. Character matters, and neither you nor anyone else can buy me."

"We both have taken great risks to come to this country, but we have different views of the elite Canadian political structure and how to function within the system. You're a novice in that regard." He paced back and forth, stopped, turned toward the front window, smiled and waved. "Ah, you have a small child who looks good in red." His grin was exaggerated.

When I looked toward the window, Mother was holding Aria on her hip. I was furious she hadn't waited in the kitchen and stood speechless as he watched for my reaction. "You leave my daughter out of this."

"I want my money now. You have this huge house, so let's go to the bank and get my money!"

I put my hand through my hair, glanced at the bodyguard, the Cadillac, and surveyed the surroundings. I didn't have any options and tried not to show the panic I felt inside. "The bank is closed, so I can't do anything today."

"You're the owner. Unlock the damn door."

"The safe is on a time lock and requires two bank officers to open, which can't happen until half-past eight tomorrow morning."

"Eng gave you money to care for Dung's brother. Where is it?"

"Eng delivered $25,000 along with Chukee, then made me return $10,000 to get my sister. The rest went for Chukee's care and burial expenses. The money was spent."

"Chukee meant nothing to me. I told Dung to eliminate him long ago." He tapped his finger against his lips and said, "Let's consider another alternative. As Dung originally proposed, sign over fifty percent interest in your bank to me."

"I won't sell, and I don't have your money." As soon as the words were out of my mouth, I knew I shouldn't have responded because whatever I said would be used against me.

"We charge interest and late fees and will provide protection which will accumulate until your debt is paid in full. You can write it off however you want, but I will get my money, fees, and interest or half interest in the bank."

Huen's bodyguard nodded toward the street. Catherine's husband, Yves, was walking along the sidewalk, and when he waved at me, Huen said, "If he takes a step toward us, he's dead," then he motioned, and his bodyguard stepped toward the railing and signaled the Cadillac. The driver-side door opened, and a stocky man got out. I held my breath and waved back at Yves, who continued walking. I wanted Yves to notice the men on the porch and in the black car, but it was too much to hope he would do that and contact the OPP.

"Tomorrow morning at nine o'clock, I'll send my men to collect either $175,000 to pay off my debt and interest or a Stock Certificate for fifty percent of Merchant's Bank stock. If you involve the police, I'll know, and at different times, one by one, we'll murder your wife, child, mother, sister, your house girl, and lastly, you." His eyes were cold and empty as he pointed at me and said, "Remember this shoemaker, like you, I'm a man of my word." Then in a flat, matter-of-fact tone, he added, "I already have insurance to assure your cooperation."

"What insurance?"

When he motioned toward the car, the front passenger side window lowered, Huen made another hand gesture, and the rear window lowered. Lijuan and Lysa were in the back seat with gags over their mouths.

Huen straightened his coat and said, "I'll have my money or stock in Merchant's Bank tomorrow, or you'll never see these two hookers again. Besides, I have work for them. They can pay back my money with their flesh."

Huen and his bodyguard walked to the Cadillac. Huen sat in the front seat, the guard in the back, and they sped away. Without being noticed, I tried to see the license plate, but my angle was poor. I rushed inside and yelled at Mother. "I told you to stay in the kitchen! Go pack a diaper bag for Aria, enough for several days. I need to get you and Aria to safety."

I picked up the phone, then slammed it on the desk. The line was dead. My head pounded as Mother stared at me in horror but didn't move. "Hurry, I'm taking you and Aria to Catherine's. I'll call the police when we get there, then I need to find Caitlin, Rhoda, and Kathleen at church."

"We can go to Rhoda's. It is closer."

"No, we can't. Huen has Lijuan and Lysa."

"What!"

"They were in the backseat of the car." Her face lost its color and her legs started to give way. I took hold of her arm to steady her and said, "We need to hurry."

I kept looking about for any cars following us as we scurried as fast as Mother could, pushing the stroller to Catherine's. I didn't want to jeopardize Catherine, Yves, or Joseph, but I didn't know what else to do.

On the way, I mulled over where I could raise $175,000 in cash, and the only person I knew who could get that much money quickly and wouldn't ask questions was Darvin Avant.

We entered Joseph's house from the kitchen, and I told Mother to take Aria upstairs to Kai and Wei Lei's loft.

"Winson, do I hear Aria's stroller?" Catherine asked from the parlor.

"We've an emergency, and I need to use the phone. Mother and Aria are on their way upstairs. Is Yves home?"

"He's out walking. Why?"

I told her about meeting Huen on the porch and seeing Yves walk in front of the house. She clutched her heart, then, with a tremble in her voice, said, "Yves is in his own world when he's working on a new musical composition, so I doubt he would recognize a threat. Would they harm him because he waved at you?"

"They don't know who he is, but I want to know he's safe. I need to call Chief Kirkpatrick, tell him what happened, and have the OPP look for Yves."

"Oh, my Lord," her voice quivered.

Holding her hand I said, "I promise Yves will be okay."

"I don't know how you can promise that, but I trust you'll do all you can."

I called the OPP and asked the operator for Chief Kirkpatrick. The operator said he wouldn't be in today but would transfer me to Sargent Ellarby, the on-duty officer. When I said I wouldn't speak to Ellarby, she asked why, and I told her he investigated me on a false rape charge and was reprimanded. She said he was currently the only officer in the station.

I raised my voice and said, "It's a life-and-death emergency. Chief Kirkpatrick is working with the RCMP to capture a criminal who showed up at my house and abducted my sister and a friend."

"Yelling at me won't help. You need to speak to the on-duty Sargent. Please hold."

"No, damn it. If you don't call the Chief, I will. My family is under threat, and my sister has been kidnapped. I won't talk to Ellarby."

Then, after a long pause, she said, "Give me your number, and I'll see what I can do."

Within five minutes, Chief Kirkpatrick called, and after I explained the situation, he asked for descriptions of the vehicle, Huen, and his bodyguard. "We'll ask for the RCMP's assistance, issue an all-points bulletin for their arrest, and set up roadblocks to stop and scrutinize all suspect outgoing traffic from Collingwood. I'll authorize unmarked patrol cars and officers to guard you, your family, and Rhoda, and we'll look for Yves."

"Huen threatened to kill my family if I contacted the police. My mother and Aria are in the loft at Joseph Lawrence's house with Kai and Wei Lei. I must get to the Baptist Church before Caitlin gets out, and she has our car."

"I'll pick you up in my personal vehicle in five minutes and send an officer in an unmarked car to stay with your family."

"Make sure it isn't Ellarby."

While waiting for the Chief, I called the phone company to restore our service. The operator told me the repair department doesn't work on weekends, and it would be a few days before service could be restored. I pleaded with her that this was an emergency, but she reiterated there were no working crews on the weekend, then she clicked off the call.

I told Catherine the police would look for Yves, and she said, "My god, Yves won't even know what danger he's exposed to."

My next call was to David Yonge. Vancouver was three hours earlier as he answered on the first ring. He gasped when I told him about the events. "They have Lysa! We must find Tai Huen today. I'll call the RCMP right away and get back to you."

"My phone line has been cut. I'll need to call you back. If the RCMP can pick up Eng on D'Arcy Island, maybe arresting him could provide leverage."

"The RCMP has been watching D'Arcy, but I haven't received any additional information." I gave him the phone number to the Lawrence house and told him he could leave messages with whoever answered.

Kai came downstairs and wanted to go with me, but I told him it would be best if he stayed to protect everyone there. I asked him to lock all the doors and not let anyone in he didn't recognize.

Chief Kirkpatrick picked me up and dropped me at the church. I went into the foyer, paced back and forth, then stepped into the back of the sanctuary and saw Caitlin near the front in the middle of a row. It was near the end of the service, so I waited by our car in the parking lot.

When Caitlin, Maureen, Kathleen, and Rhoda came outside and saw me by the car, Caitlin asked, "What are you doing here, and where's Aria?"

"She's with Kai and Wei Lei. Hurry, get in the car. We need to go."

"Did something happen to Lily?" she asked.

"All of you, in the car, and I'll tell you on the way."

When I told them about the confrontation with Tai Huen at our house and Lijuan and Lysa were taken hostage, Caitlin went crazy and screamed, "No!!!!!!" Her face turned red, her voice was stern, and the tears rolled down her cheeks as she said, "I'm taking Aria, and we're leaving! I won't have my child put in danger."

"Lijuan and Lysa were at my house! Did those mobsters break in?" Rhoda screamed.

"Please try not to panic. I've already taken Aria to a safe place."

"Nowhere in Collingwood is safe from those criminals," Caitlin said.

I've never seen her so angry. "Where will you go?"

"I'm not telling you!"

"But how am I going to protect you?"

"You haven't protected us so far and haven't helped the RCMP stop the Chinese crime ring."

"If you won't tell me where you're going, please let Catherine know you're safe. Our phone line at the house has been cut."

"What!"

There was a cold silence on the way to Joseph's house. I pulled into the driveway, Caitlin hurried out, then ran upstairs for Aria. Maureen picked up the diaper bag, and Kathleen put the stroller in the trunk while Caitlin spoke to Catherine.

Before they left, I took hold of Caitlin's arm and said, "You have every right to be angry, but I need to know you're safe. Kirkpatrick is providing undercover officers to protect us, but he needs to know where you are. Call him at home or at the

OPP station." I gave her his home phone number. "If you're going to leave town, the crime ring knows our car, so you should take Maureen's vehicle to be safe. There's an unmarked police car out front. I'll ask them to follow you to your mother's if you need to get a few things. Don't go to our house. Buy anything else you need. I put money in the diaper bag."

Her face was red, and she was uncommunicative.

"Rhoda, you shouldn't go home either. You can stay with Lily and me. We'll have police protection."

"I don't know what to do. I've been violated. Lijuan and Lysa were taken from my home, my home!"

"If you go home, lock the doors and don't let anyone in," I cautioned.

I stood alone in the driveway, watched them leave, and sensed my life falling apart. Events were out of control, and I was dependent on others. When I returned to the house, Kai suggested that Lily and I stay with them until this mess was over.

"I need to return home, but Mother, you should stay here."

"No, I will stay with you," Mother insisted.

"I appreciate that, but when I go to the bank in the morning, I want you here with Wei Lei and Kai. I won't leave you alone in the house."

"But you don't have a car," Kai said.

"I'll contact Gene, the security guard at the bank, and have him pick us up and take me back and forth. He's armed and a war veteran."

Mother went upstairs, and I called Gene at home and spoke to his daughter, who said Gene had driven his wife to her sister's house in Hamilton and would return in the morning. I would need to find other transportation.

Minutes seemed like hours, and my thoughts were hyperactive. Kai and I were sitting at the kitchen table when someone tried to open the outside door. We both jumped, Kai pulled a carving knife from a drawer, and I looked through the window, opened the door, and embraced Yves.

"To what do I owe such a warm welcome? And why is the door locked?"

"You're home safe," I replied.

"Kai, what's the knife for? Was I in danger?"

Then we heard Catherine shout from the parlor, "Yves, where have you been?"

Yves and I walked into the parlor together.

"I was working on a new arrangement and was at a musical impasse, but I worked it out this morning during my walk and then went to Leonard Stern's to let him know how I proposed to handle certain transitions. Time drifted away from us. Sorry if I caused you concern."

"I should've known. I told Winson you lose track of time when you're composing."

He looked perplexed as he kissed Catherine on her cheek and sat beside her.

I was pacing back and forth, trying not to panic. "My sister and Lysa Wu have been kidnapped. Did you notice the license number on the black Cadillac in front of my house today?"

"Was there a Cadillac? I saw you talking with two men on the porch but didn't notice their car."

I called Kirkpatrick and told him Yves was safe at home and Caitlin left town. He said she called, told him where they were going, and made him promise he wouldn't tell me where she was, so he told me not to ask. He said Caitlin put our car in her mother's garage and left the keys under the rear floor mat and that he'd have the OPP in her location have a patrol car check on her frequently.

When Joseph and Julia returned in the afternoon, I told him about the day's events and apologized for bringing trouble into his house.

"You're welcome here. Sorry, I don't have an extra bedroom for you to spend the night, but you can sleep on a couch."

"Mother is upstairs with Wei Lei. We'll stay here for a while if you don't mind." I paced about while I waited for the phone to ring. I called Rhoda's house, but there was no answer. Maybe her phone line was cut, too. I decided to call Maureen's, and Rhoda answered on the second ring.

"Rhoda, are you okay?"

"I answered the phone, so I'm not dead!"

"I'm sorry to get you involved with my syndicate issues."

"These are more than issues, they're life-threatening, and it's frightening for all of us."

"I feel terrible to have put all of you in this position."

"It's overwhelming."

"Will you be okay at Maureen's?"

"The doors are locked, and I have a baseball bat!"

"I'm at Joseph's house if you need me. Mother and I will go home later."

"If you want to stay the night here, you'll have phone service. I'll probably sleep better with you in the house."

"That's a good idea. Kai is fixing dinner. Would you like to eat?"

"I've no appetite."

David called about six and told me the RCMP had picked up Eng and seven others on D'Arcy Island. They were in custody in Vancouver, and an officer was discussing a plea bargain with Eng.

I called and updated Kirkpatrick, told him I was staying at Maureen's, and gave him her phone number and address.

Chapter Twenty-One

It was a restless night as I tried to sleep on the sofa at Maureen's and eventually dozed off but was startled awake when the phone rang, and Chief Kirkpatrick asked how I was holding up.

"I'd say miserable, but it would be an optimistic exaggeration of how I really feel. You didn't call at five in the morning to see how I am."

"Today looks to be better than yesterday."

"Is Tai Huen dead?"

"The RCMP has surrounded an abandoned church camp a couple of miles outside Clarksburg and assured me that Lysa and Lijuan are there, and there's no way for Huen and his men to escape. We're sending OPP reinforcements to assist in the capture."

"Can I drive to Clarksburg to get Lijuan and Lysa?"

"We need the element of surprise and it will be an assault, otherwise Huen will use the women as shields or hostages. If it becomes to a shootout, no one wins."

The blood left my body. My sister had gone from one trauma to another, and I had brought Lysa from a safe place where she was free from the crime ring, and into my world, and her life was endangered, and she was back in the world she hated.

"Depending on the outcome, they'll either be taken to a hospital or brought to Collingwood for debriefing. Stay near the phone, I'll be in touch."

"You realize Lijuan's mental condition is fragile. Does she need to be debriefed?"

"That's not my call, but I'll let the RCMP know to be careful with questioning her."

"How did you find them?"

"Eng spilled his guts when the Vancouver RCMP picked him up. Hopefully, this chapter of your previous life will end soon. I'll call again when I know more."

I called David and gave him Kirkpatrick's update on Huen. When I asked how he was, he said, "I've been up all night watching Eng being interrogated. When he was offered immunity, it surprised all of us when he accepted it, almost as if he wanted it. He revealed Huen's location near Clarksburg, current operations near Dawson Creek, and various business enterprises. Everyone on D'Arcy island is in custody."

"My history with Eng is complex. I begged him to leave the syndicate and am grateful he finally turned against them. Maybe he can have a better life. I hope you can get some sleep now."

"I came home to shower and pack. I'm on the six am flight to Toronto and should be in Collingwood by late afternoon. Do you have room for me?"

"Always. Caitlin left yesterday with Aria, her mother, and Kathleen. She's frightened and wants Aria far away from Huen."

"I know this has been difficult for both of you. Dealing with Tak and Dung was traumatic for Caitlin, and she'll need time to recover."

"She's been stressed with the syndicate, adjusting to my mother and Lijuan, and grieving over her father's passing. I don't know what I would have done without your help. I'm still anxious about Lijuan and Lysa because they aren't safe yet."

"Lysa is the reason I'm coming. I've been in a panic since your call yesterday and need to see that she's okay. I've grown quite fond of her and need to be with her."

Mother, Rhoda and I waited anxiously by the phone for the next several hours. When the call finally came that they were safe and on the way to Collingwood, we drove to the OPP station hoping to be there when they arrived.

It was several hours before we could take them home. Lijuan wouldn't speak to anyone, but Lysa had given us a full report. Several of Huen's men wanted to use Lijuan and Lysa for sex, but Huen restrained them. Lijuan was still traumatized, and Lysa thought they should return to Rhoda's and have time alone. Mother insisted on staying with Lijuan at Rhoda's.

I went to see Catherine and told her Lijuan and Lysa were safe, and Tai Huen and his men were in prison. When she wouldn't tell me where Caitlin was, I pleaded, "She needs to know the circumstances have changed, and the syndicate is no longer a threat to us."

"That will please her, but she has been through quite a shock, and she's like a mother bear protecting her cub. Give her time to heal. I'll tell her what happened, but wait for her to call, and don't push her."

∽

I wasn't ready to go to the bank and deal with business, so I called Peggy to let her know and then went to Clive's office and told him about Huen's arrest and Lijuan and Lysa's rescue.

"This could be a setback for Lijuan. How is she handling this?"

"Lysa asked to give her time alone with Lijuan. She wasn't talking when I picked them up at the OPP and took them to Rhoda's."

"Do you want to speak with Bitsy?"

"I'm a mess, but maybe another day."

"How about we change the subject, and I give you an update on Taylor and Avant?"

"I hope it's good news."

"We petitioned Judge Ravenwood's court for Taylor's stock as partial settlement for the unconscionable loss suffered by Merchant's Bank and unjust enrichment. We also petitioned for an injunction to prevent Avant's participation in standard shareholder entitlements, including attending shareholder meetings, reviewing financial information, and receiving shareholder distributions. If distributions are made, Merchants Bank would need to set aside the money for Taylor's shares until the court renders an opinion."

"So we're seeking judgment from the court and asserting Taylor has damaged us, and Merchants Bank is requesting Taylor's stock as partial redress?"

"Correct, we're asserting the stock transfer to Avant was fraudulent and requesting the stock as partial restitution. We're hoping for a pre-trial judgment concluding a fraudulent transfer was made by Taylor to Avant in an effort to hide assets from a creditor, and our suit for a default judgment for damages against Taylor be approved. Avant's attorney sent a scalding rebuttal letter, but they have no grounds to prevail."

"So whatever was done in the dark will now come to the light?"

"Not yet, but we're headed in the right direction. I've also filed reports with the Office of the Inspector General of Banks and Miss Jerome's office."

I was pleased with the news, but I was preoccupied with Caitlin. Before leaving Clive's office, I called the phone company and was able to schedule the repair of my phone lines in the afternoon. The repair crew arrived shortly after I returned home, and I had phone service within two hours. My first call was to Catherine to see if she had heard from Caitlin, and I was relieved when Catherine gave me the phone number for Caitlin's Aunt in Windsor, Ontario.

When I called, Caitlin said, "Chief Kirkpatrick told me about capturing Huen and his men. Since Tak and Dung are dead and Huen and his men are in custody, are we finally rid of them?"

"I hope so. I'm so sorry for my blind spots and apologize for all I've put you through." She was silent. "I mourned the loss of my family in China, but that doesn't compare to a future without you and Aria."

"Your 'I hope so' doesn't sound certain, and I'm not ready to return home. I'm putting Aria first, not you and me. You said the trafficking ring is like getting tar on you, which won't come off, and there's never just one roach in the kitchen." There was nothing I could say, and I remained silent as she continued, "Are we going to be like Lysa, always looking over our shoulders and feeling like we've a shadow hovering over us?"

"A shadow can scare you but cannot hurt you. The RCMP and OPP are confident they have, or will have soon, everyone from the crime ring in custody."

"I don't like the word, soon. How can they be sure? When Dung died, Huen took over, and now, who will replace him?"

"Did Kirkpatrick tell you that he thought this should terminate their organization?"

She didn't answer.

"Almost everyone deals with something from their past. So where does faith enter? You have said we need to trust God with our lives and future."

"I don't know if you even believe in God."

I was at a loss. Did I believe in God, or was I only throwing words in her face? "I know you believe in God, and I believe in you and want to believe in God, and I'm praying that God will bring you and Aria home and all of our troubles with the crime ring are over. All I know for certain is that I'll be here whenever you're ready to come home."

I was thankful when David arrived because I didn't want to be alone. We both went to see Lijuan and Lysa. Rhoda had prepared dinner, and Lijuan joined us and talked, but not about the events of the last two days. David couldn't keep his eyes off Lysa and asked if she would walk with him after dinner. They returned holding hands and smiling, and he had lipstick on his collar.

~

Ten days later, I was in the kitchen when the back door opened, and Caitlin walked in with Aria, who was wiggling to get out of her arms. Caitlin put her on the floor, and she crawled straight for her cabinet. We stood at a distance, looking at each other.

"Love, I hope you're here to stay."

"Mother kept reminding me that I married a wonderful, merciful man and asked why I couldn't forgive you." She paused and took several dry swallows, then said, "You didn't ask to be trafficked, and none of what we've experienced was your fault. Mother has always stood up for you, even if Daddy didn't. But even Daddy admired how you stood on principle."

Aria banged the cabinet door open and shut.

Caitlin smiled and said, "Over the past week, my emotions, the anger and the grief building inside me since Daddy's death, flooded out, and I cried until my bones ached. Mother held me and reminded me to listen to my heart, not Daddy whispering to me from the grave."

When she put her arms around me, I said, "Welcome home. I'll thank Maureen when I see her."

Caitlin kissed me firmly, a kiss promising so much more.

∽

I hoped the events which started twenty years ago in China were behind us; nonetheless, I decided to let tomorrow worry about itself.

Addendum

D'Arcy Island

In *Burden of Conscience*, D'Arcy Island was used as a setting for one of Dung's crime ring operations and, in reality, was part of the history of anti-Chinese racism in Canada.

D'Arcy is two islands lying about three nautical miles off the east coast of the Saanich Peninsula north of Victoria. Cobble beaches and Douglas Fir forests, and Arbutus trees cover the island. All this beauty, however, hides a much darker past. D'Arcy island was once a Leper Colony.

In 1891 five Chinese people with leprosy were discovered in a shack in Chinatown. The traditional horror of leprosy and perhaps a degree of racism sparked the municipal council of the day to take quick action. Hoping to contain the disease and prevent panic, the municipal government established a secret settlement on D'Arcy Island to quarantine and care for the patients. It was not a secret for long, as the story was soon leaked to local newspapers. By May 20, 1891, they obtained approval from the province to establish a colony on D'Arcy island and sent over a crew of men to construct the necessary facilities. The settlement operated from 1891-1924 and housed 49 patients; however, these sick individuals were left there to fend for themselves with no medical care, and many of them were weak from leprosy and had to bury their own dead. They had to collect their own water, which was seriously lacking during the summer months. Their only relief was a supply boat delivering supplies every three months, along with a medical officer to check on their condition. Conditions on the island remained deplorable until 1905 when the Provincial Government finally became involved and convinced the federal government to provide financing. In 1906 the federal government passed the Leprosy Act, and the colony became a medical facility with new buildings and a caretaker. Perhaps, more importantly, a new attitude towards people with leprosy resulted in a repatriation of a few of the residents back to China and the necessary medicines to alleviate their suffering. The facilities at D'Arcy were permanently closed in 1924.

Renisa Mawani, a sociology professor at the University of British Columbia, said, "This handling of Chinese lepers was one of several anti-Chinese policies Canada implemented during this time. White patients in Canada's other leper colony in Tracadie, N.B., were cared for by doctors and nuns. But on D'Arcy Island, the men were essentially left to die. A stigma was already associated with the disease, but what we saw with D'Arcy Island was racism becoming a significant part of the stigma. British Columbia didn't have a large white population, so there was this concern about the fragility and the instability of the white community on the West Coast."

This was a period when anti-Chinese racism was legalized in Canada through the Chinese Head Tax in 1885, followed by the Chinese Exclusion Act in 1923. With growing calls to restrict and ultimately prohibit migration from China, leprosy became a disease strongly associated with Chinese migration. D'Arcy Island was part of a broader atmosphere of anti-Chinese racism aimed at securing B.C. as a space of whiteness.

https://sociology.ubc.ca/news-tag/darcy-island/

https://en.wikipedia.org/wiki/D%27Arcy_Island

https://www.timescolonist.com/life/victoria-banished-chinese-lepers-to-island-colony-4560261

Addendum

Douglas Jung

The character of David Yonge in *Burden of Conscience* was influenced by the life of Douglas Jung, the first Chinese Canadian elected to the House of Commons.

Jung's triumph was remarkable; few voters in Vancouver Centre had shared his Progressive Conservative sympathies in a recent election, and fewer still shared his ethnic heritage.

Every advance in Jung's career seems to have been a marker in Canada's history of race relations. He was the first Chinese Canadian to be accepted to the British Columbia bar; the first to appear before the B.C. Court of Appeals, the highest court in the province; the first to be elected to Parliament; the first to represent Canada at the United Nations.

He was a trailblazer in the land of his birth, a man of sharp intellect and ambition who came of age as Canadian society began dismantling legally sanctioned racism.

In 1944, when his own country considered him to be less than a full citizen, Jung risked his life by volunteering for duty as a saboteur behind Japanese lines. As a veteran, he, at last, earned the right to vote. After his election, he campaigned to redress the wrongs committed against fellow Chinese Canadians.

Douglas Jung was born in Victoria on Feb. 25, 1924. His father, Vick Ching Jung, an immigrant of humble means from Guangdong Province in China, named him after Douglas Street, the city's main thoroughfare. He was the youngest of three sons. His birth came eight months after the implementation of the Chinese Immigration (Exclusion) Act on July 1, 1923, which essentially closed Canada's doors. The date came to be known as "Humiliation Day" in the Chinatown ghettos. He inherited a world where property covenants forbade him from buying land in many neighborhoods. He was barred from pharmacy, medicine, and the law. He sat in segregated movie houses and was barred from swimming at certain pools.

Jung completed his public school education at Victoria High School as the Second World War raged. He enlisted soon after the Canadian government reversed a policy barring Chinese Canadians from serving in the armed forces. The British wanted to recruit soldiers of Chinese background who could be sent into Asian jungles to blend in with the local population as secret agents. Jung volunteered for clandestine warfare and was sent to isolated Commando Bay near Penticton, B.C., for intense training in demolition, sabotage and silent killing. "We looked like cutthroats," Jung recalled in Unwanted Soldiers, a 1999 National Film Board documentary. "We were not in military uniforms. We were unshaven, disheveled." Jung, a sergeant, belonged to Force 136 of the British-led Special Operations Executive. His perilous assignment was to organize resistance behind Japanese lines. He was equipped with a suicide pill, which was to be taken to avoid torture should he be captured. As a spy, capture meant death. "We were prepared to risk our lives for nothing," Jung said. "There was no guarantee the Canadian government was going to give us the full rights of Canadian citizenship. We were taking a gamble." Both his brothers also served. Arthur Jung piloted a Lancaster on bombing missions over occupied Europe, while

Ross Jung served in a medical unit. The war ended not long after Douglas Jung parachuted into the Borneo jungle.

He returned to British Columbia in 1946, taking advantage of veterans' benefits to complete a Bachelor of Arts and a law degree at the University of British Columbia. In 1947, the provincial government ended restrictions on voting for Chinese Canadians. The same year, the federal government revoked its discriminatory immigration laws, although it would be another two decades before large-scale immigration from Asia would be permitted. Jung, who continued to serve in the militia as a captain, began practice as a lawyer after graduating in 1953. He was a dapper man, rarely seen without a tie and jacket, his black hair carefully groomed and precisely parted on the left side.

He made his electoral debut as a Conservative candidate in a provincial by-election held on Jan. 9, 1956. Jung finished a respectable second, a moral victory. His candidacy was the first by a Chinese Canadian for a seat in any Canadian legislature. Seventeen months later, he became a member of Parliament in a shocking upset.

Jung said he had become a Conservative because he could never support a party discriminating against his people. The 1958 Canadian Parliamentary Guide notes: "First M.P. of Chinese extraction." Diefenbaker sent Jung to the United Nations as Canada's representative to the Legal Committee.

"I took my place there," he once told the Vancouver Sun, "and an usher came over and said, 'I'm sorry, sir, but this seat is for the Canadian delegation.' " Jung replied, "I am the Canadian delegation." He won re-election by a massive 10,117 votes in the Diefenbaker landslide of 1958. That same year he was elected national president of his party's youth wing.

However, Jung caused a stir when he said he wanted to visit China, which had fallen under Communist control. The issue was controversial in the Chinese Canadian community, which he once described as his best ally and harshest critic.

On Dec. 6, 1958, he married Joy Calderwood, but their union ended in divorce.

As an MP, Jung proved to be an indefatigable advocate. He convinced the government to grant an amnesty to those Chinese who came to Canada under false names. He also helped to create the National Productivity Council, now known as the Economic Council of Canada. Jung lost his seat in 1962 to Liberal J. R. Nicholson, an industrialist who was a pillar of the establishment and would later serve as B.C. lieutenant-governor. After Conservatives lost elections in 1963 and 1965, Jung bowed out as a candidate and ran a successful legal practice specializing in immigration issues for many years.

https://en.wikipedia.org/wiki/Douglas_Jung

http://vichigh.com/wp-content/uploads/2013/09/Jung-Douglas-41.pdf

https://www.ccmms.ca/veteran-stories/army/douglas-jung/

https://burmastarmemorial.org/archive/stories/1405898-biography-of-captain-douglas-jung-soa? https://chinatown.library.uvic.ca/sites/default/files/Interviews/Interview_Chinese_Veterans_Association.pdf

https://www.ccmms.ca/veteran-stories/army/henry-albert-hank-wong/

https://www.huffpost.com/archive/ca/
entry/chinese-canadian-veterans-force-136_
ca_5ccc68a4c4b01da999112633

https://canadianmilitaryhistory.ca/chinese-canadian-secret-
warriors-in-the-pacific/ http://rusiviccda.org/wp-content/
uploads/2017/02/We_were_dead_once_we_flew_into_
Burma_-_Chinese_Canadians_in_Force_136_-_Trevor_
Gallagher.pdf

https://www.theglobeandmail.com/life/first-person/
article-my-uncle-was-a-canadian-chinese-soldier-his-story-is-
colourful/

Addendum

Ellen Fairclough

The character of Miss Ellen Jerome in *Burden of Conscience* was influenced by the life of Ellen Fairclough. A pioneering politician, Ellen Louks Fairclough became Canada's first female federal cabinet minister in 1957, and was later appointed Secretary of State.

Jerome became involved with the Conservative Party and was elected to the House of Commons in 1950. Despite the absence of female role models in the political sphere, Ellen forged ahead to develop a successful political career and served as Minister of Citizenship and Immigration, Minister for Indian Affairs, and Postmaster General.

A trailblazer in a world of male-dominated politics, she gave about 150 speeches a year in the House of Commons and fought for equal pay for work of equal value. Ellen also worked with the Girl Guides, the Consumers' Association of Canada, and many charities.

On Canada Day in 1992, Queen Elizabeth II bestowed on Ellen Fairclough the title of "Right Honourable", almost 30 years after she left Parliament, recognizing her life achievements. She was elected to the House of Commons five times, a record unmatched by any other woman during the 1950s and 1960s. In addition, she was responsible for Indian Affairs when, in 1960, Aboriginal Canadians were given the right to vote.

https://www.thecanadianencyclopedia.ca/en/article/ellen-fairclough

http://www.heroines.ca/people/fairclough.html

https://www.elections.ca/content.
aspx?section=res&dir=cim/issue7&document=p7&lang=e

Acknowledgments

A heartfelt thank you to my wonderful wife, Karen, for her willingness to review, comment, discuss, restructure, and for her significant contributions to help formulate and write the story, and for her constant and steadfast encouragement and love. She brought love into my life from our first kiss.

To Dr. Lew Spurlock for his friendship, literary guidance, and mentorship, which has furthered my journey as an author.

I also want to thank my many gifted proofreading and editing partners, who graciously provided constructive criticism and encouragement. And thanks to Sarah Maldonado for her legal research.

Thanks to Travis Novitsky for permission to use one of his breathtaking photos, *"Early Riser's Delight.,"* for the book cover.

About the Author

George Fillis is an internationally known author of the Collingwood Series whose works are featured in Midwest Book Review and California Book Watch. A graduate of Trinity University, he lives in San Antonio, Texas, with his wife, Karen.

He discovered his passion for writing after careers in securities, real estate, and biotech. Then, inspired by travels to China and Canada, he heard a remarkable love story about a 'Paper Son,' which was the seed for the Collingwood Series.

He hopes this series generates awareness about what it means to stand alone in the face of overwhelming odds, the importance of character, always choosing to do what is right, and understanding what living outside one's comfort zone means. All of which come at a cost.

Made in the USA
Las Vegas, NV
09 July 2023

74424684R00156